120 MILLION

120 MILLION

By

MICHAEL GOLD

Short Story Index Reprint Series

 BOOKS FOR LIBRARIES PRESS
FREEPORT, NEW YORK

First Published 1929
Reprinted 1971

INTERNATIONAL STANDARD BOOK NUMBER:
0-8369-4039-3

LIBRARY OF CONGRESS CATALOG CARD NUMBER:
77-178438

PRINTED IN THE UNITED STATES OF AMERICA
BY
NEW WORLD BOOK MANUFACTURING CO., INC.
HALLANDALE, FLORIDA 33009

CONTENTS

		PAGE
Foreword	. . . .	7

Proletarian Sketches

CHAPTER
I.	COAL BREAKER	. . . .	11
II.	GOD IS LOVE	. . . .	16
III.	THE DAMNED AGITATOR	. . . . .	33
IV.	THE PASSWORD TO THOUGHT—TO CULTURE		44
V.	THE AMERICAN FAMINE	. . . . .	60
VI.	DEATH OF A NEGRO	. . . . . .	72
VII.	FREE!	. . . .	80
VIII.	BOUND TO GET HOME	. . . . .	88
IX.	TWO MEXICOS	. . . . . .	94
X.	ON A SECTION GANG	. . . . .	115
XI.	LOVE ON A GARBAGE DUMP	. . . .	123
XII.	FASTER, AMERICA, FASTER!	. . . . .	135

Proletarian Chants and Recitations

XIII.	THE STRANGE FUNERAL IN BRADDOCK	. .	145
XIV.	BIG JOE'S BIRTHDAY	. . . . . .	149
XV.	THIRD DEGREE	. . . .	152
XVI.	THE GIRL BY THE RIVER	. . . .	155
XVII.	A GREAT DEED WAS NEEDED	. . .	159
XVIII.	STRIKE!	. . . .	170
XIX.	VANZETTI IN THE DEATH HOUSE	. . .	184
XX.	*120 Million*	. . . .	191

FOREWORD

THE *sketches of proletarian American life in this book were written mostly from my 19th to 26th year, and are arranged in the order of composition.*

Melancholy runs through them, lifting to militant courage in the last part of the book.

I have outgrown the melancholy, but feel it was perhaps inevitable in the progress of a proletarian writer.

Youth is not always brave; often it is bewildered. Poverty crushes us in youth; we can see no escape, we are isolated and suicidal. Our revolt then is individual and subjective; we write with lyric pain out of loneliness.

But the adolescent fog clears, giving way to the bold outlines of reality.

One learns that others, too, are caught in the cosmic trap of poverty; and that out of despair, melancholy, and helpless rage of millions, a world movement has been born, to abolish poverty.

Mass is strength, mass is clarity and courage.

From ego-poet to mass-poet is the usual path of the proletarian writer.

The old Christian Socialist literature was written by members of the upper class. It portrayed the worker with the pity, condescension and prayer of a charity lady or slummer.

The worker was rarely portrayed as a human

being, but as some strange brute savage living in the subcellars of life.

When a Robert Burns appeared, or a Maxim Gorky or Jack London, he was eyed with wonder, as if a truck horse should suddenly sing opera.

The situation has changed. No one can patronize the workers any longer. Their advance guard are not victims, but fearless soldiers in the world war against poverty.

They ask for nothing they cannot take.

Thousands of writers have appeared to express the new proletariat; a literary generation bred in factories, mines and slums of every land, writing boldly and dynamically of the life they know.

No more slumming or missionary pity.

Proletarian literature now dominates many lands. It is the main current in Soviet Russia, it is one of two main streams in Japanese thought. It is strong in China and India, and strong in Germany and Middle Europe.

One finds it bursting into the parlors of British and French literature. There is a great gale of it in Latin-America. Symptoms appear even in our bourgeois United States, last fort of capitalism.

Note that nearly all young proletarian writers to-day are Communists. My own visit to Soviet Russia, and contact with its new life and art, gave me the sense of direction I had needed. Soviet Russia cured me of sentimentality, and gave me courage to persist in a land where the proletarian writer has no friends.

The workers' chants and recitations in the back

of this book were inspired by things learned in Soviet Russia.

The poets there have socialized the aristocratic art of poetry. Their theory is that poetry should be useful. It should organize the emotion of the Revolution, as political leaders organize the intellect.

Poetry is used in Soviet Russia as a means of welding the masses into solidarity.

It is chanted at mass-meetings, it furnishes new rituals. The Soviet poets have restored poetry to its primitive Homeric utilities.

I have written the first mass-recitation in this country, I believe, and some of the first workers' chants. I hope others will write them, too. They are needed.

The Social Revolution in this country is a wheat-kernel fighting through stony soil. It is a beginning. My book is a beginning, too.

I dedicate it to my comrades, the few, brave, scattered proletarian writers of America.

Let us persist.

COAL BREAKER

ALWAYS between the sky and their earth the miners saw the unhallowed, grim, irregular mass of the coal-breaker, a tall structure black with dust, ugly as a giant toad. It dominated the whole valley.

There were green trees in that valley, meadows and flowers for the light to kindle in the summer days. The spring brought a soft flush there, much as in other parts of the world. There were stars and moon at night, the sun by day.

There was beauty, but it lived furtively under a shadow. A great somber coal-mine was in that valley. It had dragged its black, slimy trail across the clear brightness of nature. A town of dirty, sad houses was heaped about like stacks of filth on the grass of the valley level. Huge hills of slag stood about the mine's mouth, mounds of darkness from which spurted jets of diabolical flame.

The men of all the races lived in the houses of the town. They shuffled in the morning through the muddy streets toward the mine-pit, and returned in the dusk with their emptied dinner pails, their faces black as sinister masks, their bodies dripping sweat, and stooped in weary curves.

Saturday nights there was one brief candle of romance lit in this dark reality of toil. The miners drew their pay then, and spent some of it on liquor.

They danced, they sang, they fought and grew sentimental, they remembered for a moment their human heritage of play.

I was in Miduvski's general store on a night such as this. The place was dimly lit by lamps, and Miduvski, a big, bald-headed shrewd speculator, stood plotting behind his counter. There were a few odd customers lounging about. Nothing happened for an hour or so; then some of the miners came trooping in.

There were about eight of them, and a few boys who worked in the coal-breaker trailed admiringly in the rear. The miners were dressed in overalls and black caps with tiny lamps fastened on them, and these lamps seemed like the horns of a group of wild-faced devils. The men were of all races, most of them short and squarely built. Their white teeth flashed out of the gloom of their faces as they laughed uproariously, for they were all a little drunk.

"Set 'em up, Miduvski!" shouted one, a stout, powerful man with a merry black face and little Chinese eyes. "The kid here is treating!"

He dragged forward a youngster who was no more than ten years old, and who was dressed in ragged overalls too long for him, and a miner's cap that came over his ears. The boy had high cheekbones, and coal dust darkened his straight nose and sandy hair of a young Slav.

"The little Hunyak is goin' to treat!" roared the stout miner again. "This is his first week in the breaker, and he's celebratin'. Ainchyer, kid?"

"Yeh!" the boy said, laughing mirthlessly and

staring at them all with big, dazed eyes. "I'm a man now!"

At this there was a general outbreak of laughter, and one of the men clapped the boy approvingly on the shoulder. Miduvski filled the glasses with whisky, which they gulped down with great smacking of lips and long "Ah-h-hs!"

"Give the kid a hooker too!" shouted a tall, reckless Irishman, pounding on the counter. "He's one of us now, by gorry!"

"Yes, yes!" cried the other men, and the storekeeper poured another glass of the red, fiery stuff, which the boy swallowed mechanically.

"Yah!" shouted the men admiringly, "that's the idea!"

They watched the boy take out his pay envelope and extract a dollar bill which he laid on the counter.

"Game to the core!" the Irishman said, slapping the boy on the back again. "Let's have another now! My treat!"

The boy leaned against the counter, and looked about him foolishly. "I ain't goin' to be a miner all my life," he announced, with a superior air. "I'm goin' to be a doctor!"

"Hooray for Jansy!" the men shouted, reaching out for the newly-filled glasses.

The boy drank with them again, with a careless pride on his young face. But the next moment, the wide store with its shadows of lamplight, its dark, deep corners and laden shelves, grew dim and whirling to his eyes. He felt like rushing out into the fragrant country night, to fling himself down on the cool grass somewhere, and to breathe pure air. A miner offered him a chew of tobacco, and the boy thought it necessary to stuff the vile brown plug in his mouth, and to munch it busily. But he was sick to the pit of his stomach.

A small boy had crept shyly into the place, and was looking at the scene with fear. He came over finally and timidly plucked the young worker by the sleeve.

"Jansy," he said, "Mommer's lookin' for ye everywhere, and she says she'll give ye an awfil lickin' if ye don't come right home. She's waitin' fer yer pay!"

The breaker-boy pushed his young brother away with a silly smile. "Beat it!" he said haughtily, though reeling and sick with the tobacco and rotgut whisky. "I'm a man now. Just tell Mommer I'm a man now!"

The smaller boy drew back in fright, and stood staring at his brother from the doorway, doubtful as to what to do.

"Hooray fer Jansy!" the men shouted in glee, lifting the boy on their shoulders. "Game to the core!"

"We'll have to get him a girl to-night!" the Irishman cried waving his glass of whisky recklessly. "He's a real man now, the little Polak, workin', drinkin', chewin', and whorin'!"

The boy grinned wearily. Outside in the night could be seen the monstrous form of the breaker in whose black bowels gangs of children slaved in fierce

Coal Breaker

silence ten hours each day, sorting the slag from the coal with raw fingers. The coal-breaker dominated the town, it blotted out the night and stars from human eyes. Its dust darkened all the houses and rested heavily on the weeds struggling about the mine's mouth, and in that valley even childhood was fouled and withered by the black, black dust of the breaker.

GOD IS LOVE

Poverty had imprisoned nine old men in a shaky loft downtown and had sentenced them to addressing envelopes forever. Endless, sickening envelopes they were, white and flat and inane, to be addressed with squeaky pens in the fierce and gloomy silence which attends all piece work.

A perpetual grimy twilight hung to the old loft. Brownish air and light came from a moldering airshaft; the walls were once white; spider-webs floated like banners of evil from the dusty rafters. Sometimes it rained or snowed in the strange world outside, and then the stale-green old ceiling ran with great, blistery drops.

The pens squealed, often one of the old men broke into a fit of spitting, the spiders wove and plotted their malicious snares in the caverns of the room. And this is all that ever happened in the old loft. It was a horrible cell for innocent "lifers."

Seven of the old men had adapted themselves to this trap poverty had set for their old age. They had always been meek, and so now they found nothing new to revolt against. But the other two old men possessed what are commonly termed "souls," and therefore they were unhappy.

One of these two was a fine, red-cheeked old oak of a man, who had once been a sailor. Rheumatism had cheated him out of an honorable death on the waves, and here he was now, diddling with pen and ink for a livelihood.

He was huge and strong, with great tattooed fists and arms, and a head like one of those giant crags that are lifted in defense by the land against avaricious surfs. His mass of hair was white and wild as spray, and he had blue, far-seeing eyes, colored deep by the skies and seas they had known.

He was a heavy drinker, because he needed something in which to plunge the hate he had for the loft and its fungous atmosphere. For he had been fashioned for heroism and deeds, for the open air. He grew sick for the swing of a deck under his feet, for the sharp kiss of brine on his face, for the free winds, tremendous skies, all the drama and strife of the great seas.

Sundays he would sit on a bench at the Battery and look out to the Atlantic with the eyes of a lover, his heart big with loneliness for the deep, broken waters. In the loft, he never spoke to the others, but dreamed as he scribbled of strange ports lying in exotic sunshine, of gales and the rank songs of sailormen, of women and fierce moonlight, of the creaking perfumed cordage of the tops'l schooner. . . . He hated the loft and the city with the consuming hate of a caged lion. He was drunk every night, and some of the days. . . .

The other old man dreamed of God. . . . At one time he had been a minister, and what is more, a minister who truly sought God. He had been unfrocked many years back after a lascivious woman of his congregation had snared him into "sin," he never knew how. He had been glad to find a refuge in the bleak fog of New York's underworld after the scandal. The shameful lot of dish-washing and porter jobs and begging he had regarded as a penance and cross, and he had hugged his sorrows to him in an ecstasy of atonement.

But latterly he was beginning to doubt. The exaltation was leaving him, and the chill of reality was settling down. He sometimes dared to imagine that he had long since expiated his crime, and he wondered why God demanded more of him.

Some nights he would wake and sweat with terror to think that perhaps there was no God of justice. He would reach out as if to catch something that was slipping from him. . . .

"My God, my God, why art Thou forsaking me?" he would weep into his hard, lousy pillow at the lodging house. And there would be only the nauseous smell of the bed-bugs and the swinish snores of the men in the silence. . . .

Yet all things are finally answered, and it was through the other old man with a "soul" that the minister got his own terrible reply and sign from the heavens. He was going home in the enfolding gloom and scarlet of an October twilight, a little, round-shouldered old man in a flappy old suit, an umbrella and reading matter in his embarrassed clutch. . . . One knew him for the typical failure of the cities, the amiable, unmilitant kind of a man who has love for man and beast in his watery blue eyes, and is so social that there is no place for him in society. . . .

The other old man with a soul, the sailor, had not come to work that day. . . . He was probably on another spree, and the minister got to thinking wistfully of him. He also thought of God, and this with the dim, cool mystic autumn winds in the twilight conspired to make him very melancholy. . . . It was all so sad, the huge, cryptic sky, the winds out of nowhere, the dying summer and the purposeless throngs of workers. The great tenements hung black and solemn against the last silver stains of light, and somebody was singing in a window. . . .

And then the old minister suddenly met his fellow-toiler, the old sailor of the loft. The sailor was staggering out of a glaring, hiving saloon, his head lolling and his brave old eyes blurred with drink. He was very drunk, and very helpless, and the old minister came up and talked to him.

"Good evening, brother," he said, taking the other's loose hand in his own. The sailor looked at him stupidly and muttered, "Hello."

"I missed you at the loft to-day," the minister said, gradually edging the other away from the saloon door.

"Yeh, I wasn't feeling so good," the sailor mumbled out of his confused mind. He swayed a little, and hiccoughed. "Come an' have a drink," he stammered thickly.

The minister did not answer, but took a bolder grip on the other's arm, and insinuated him down the street. The old sailor had lost his hat, and his beautiful pure white head was a knightly plume against the somber twilight. His clothes were dusty, and he had also been stripped of his collar and tie. All the fools of the city turned and looked after the two old men as they trod a complicated way through the traffic. The fools wagged their heads sagely, and clacked their tongues.

A hurdy-gurdy shot the night through with music, and the old sailor broke into a few flinging bars of the hornpipe, moving with that mechanical gayety which is so pitiful in old drunkards. He meekly stopped when the minister begged him to, and was meek until the two came to the next corner, where another teeming saloon gave off a great glitter.

Here he balked flatly, and would go no further. He wormed himself stubbornly out of the clutch of the frail little minister, and dragged to the door.

"Must have a drink," he repeated again and again in a sullen passion. He shook the minister's appealing grasp off him, and stumbled violently through the saloon door. There was a hum of raucous voices, the swift, hot breath of whisky, sour beer and tobacco, the bluff welcome of the bartender.

Then the little minister was alone. He grew very sad again, for he had dreamed of rescuing the other from a night of degradation. He wandered vaguely down Ninth Avenue, wondering whether he ought to go home now and leave the sailor to his chances. And the life of the city night smote in on his thoughts and submerged them in its great surf of movement.

The sound and fury of the city night! The elevated roared like an aroused monster overhead; the people stirred and sifted in black masses on the sidewalks; peddlers barked, pianos jangled, light flowed in golden sheets from gaudy store windows; three young girls fled with locked arms down the street, laughing and screaming with joy as three lads pursued them. Chatter, gabble, laughter, hardness, fluidity, on and on the hosts poured, as if this were all of life, raising their complex and titanic anthem of nothingness to the sky!

The old minister looked at the sky and fell to thinking of God again, and so grew sadder and sadder. He thought how alien the sky was over this brick and mortar, how intrusive the stars in the lives of these pushing, screaming people. There was no God of justice, for there was no justice. There was only pain and futility. The sky was a pitiless, needless mystery. There was a void behind its curtain, but no God. What sign was there of a God in the world?

The old man moved in the city night, his soul falling endlessly in bottomless gulfs of negation. And then, fevered and overwrought, he almost fainted when there came to his simple imagination what seemed to him a miraculous answer to his questions.

Sitting on the garbage-laden step of a tenement he beheld a slum mother nursing her infant. There was a light on her face from a nearby store window, but to the old minister it was divinity. His heart melted for love of them both—the famished, ground-down mother, the helpless, trusting child. . . .

"Love," murmured the old minister ecstatically. "God is love!"

He stood and looked at them long and long, his eyes great and shining. He thought of the life of the mother—how her days were a cycle of woes, and her moments breathed in constant pain. She lived in a pit of despair, and yet she loved. She loved and sacrificed because something moved in her that was divine—something that was God.

It was God. In the life of man God had ever been, even as He was here now on this ash-heap of poverty. God was wherever men died for an ideal, wherever mothers hovered over the babes for whom they had paid in blood and agony.

God was strong. He lived where all else seemed to have died. He stirred men to deeds that were superhuman; He gave weak women a power that was above empires. Yes, God was in the world! He was a flame that lit up the dark marshes of poverty, oppression, and pain. God was love!

It was clear now. And one must love in order to know God.

So the old minister searched his heart, and found that he had not loved the world and his fellow-men for many a month. He had almost come to hate, and that was why God had seemed to fail him. He must love again! He must love his fellow-men at the lodging house, the bestial, rum-soaked men who swore so terribly! He must love the silent and soulless men who worked with him at the addressing loft! He must love the fate which had thrust him into these sordid, foul-smelling scenes, for this was his cross, and he must learn to love even his cross!

Love! He would go back to the old sailor and

rescue that other drifting life by the power of love. He would go back to the saloon and convince the men there of God, convince them by the love overflowing from his heart and eyes.

So he went back under the bellowing elevated to the saloon. Squalling with light, it was the brightest, most beckoning spot in the dark wilderness of the streets. But its confident hard glare brought all his ingrained shyness up to defeat him. He walked timidly up to the doors and peeped into the noisy stew of the saloon. Dim in a bank of tobacco smoke he could see the great white head of his sailor friend, also the rough, cruel faces of a rout of other men. Suddenly he knew that he could not go in there and speak of love. He went back to the sidewalk and waited for the sailor to come out.

The city night closed in and owned him again. It moved fitfully about him with its turmoil, with its cats and babies and sweaty, hard-bitted men and women. He studied a fly-specked whisky advertisement in the saloon window for more than fifteen minutes. It pictured in poisonous green-and-blue "The Old Kentucky Home." The old man thought it beautiful, and it made him homesick for the soft fields of Ohio from whence he had been exiled.

A foul old woman came up and talked to him. She was dirty and leering, and she proposed a horrible thing to him. But he could almost kiss her for love, for as he noted her smirched dress and repulsive, smutty face there came to him the thought of his dear, new-found God of love. . . . How beautiful He made everything. . . .

Then the old man grew lonely for a while. He read a newspaper by the saloon's brilliant glow. An hour passed, and the old sailor did not appear. . . . The old man paced the street in front of the saloon restlessly, almost impatiently, but could not bring himself to the point of going away. . . . Something stronger than himself held him there . . . God.

And then finally the old sailor did come. The saloon doors opened outward with a crash, and through them lurched the impotent hulk of the befuddled old sailor. He could hardly stand, and a mean, city-faced bartender stood behind him and pushed the big, unyielding form with contempt and righteous exasperation.

"Out of here, you old bum," he sneered, shoving. "Out before I clip ye one. . . . Ye've made enough gab to-night for such an old son-of-a-bitch. We run a decent, respectable saloon, we do, and I'll have ye know it. . . . Out!"

The sailor looked at him glazy-eyed and unknowing. He resisted automatically, only because he was stubborn of temperament. Dully he would try again and again to push back into the barroom, and every time he did so, the bartender would kick him in the stomach and send him sodden to the sidewalk. Four times this happened, the old man muttering stupidly all the while. Once in the four times he hit the side of his cheek on the pavement, and it burst open, bleeding copiously.

The minister wrung his hands and tried to interfere, but the sailor thrust him aside. A group of people gathered, but none of them tried to stop the spectacle. Then at last the old sailor was too weak to get up, and lay writhing in the street.

The bartender cast a last withering look at him, and spat with slow scorn at the twisted form.

"It's guys like you that give a black eye to the saloon business," he said bitterly, as he went inside.

Then the old minister elbowed forward and bent over his friend. With difficulty he lifted the heavy body to its feet, while every one eyed him curiously and even cynically. His meager muscles strained as he supported the old sailor, but his heart was torn even more for the other's humiliation. . . . The old sailor went with him feebly, like a sick child, mumbling weak complaints. . . .

He would take him to his room, and let him sleep there while he himself walked the streets for the night. . . . In the morning he would come back and talk to him, and help him. . . . The old minister went out in a great flood of pity to the other. . . . The sailor must be given Love, and he must be taught to know God. . . .

They walked a few blocks in this nightmare fashion, in the hum of the avenue. The old sailor drew a little out of his stupor, and all the evil of the alcohol in him began to speak. He stopped flat in his tracks before a garish window in which candies and fruits were displayed, and made as if to punch the glass in with his hand, shouting.

The minister pulled him insistently away, saying gentle, soothing things all the while. But the sailor was half-crazy now, and he tried to shake himself free of the other again and again. He grew impatient and querulous with the minister.

"Who in hell are you anyway?" he demanded. "I don't know you. Lemme go."

"I am your brother," the old minister would say gently. "I want to take you to my room where you can be safe and sleep till morning."

And over and over again with sickening insistence the old sailor would answer, "You ain't my brother. You're a thief, that's what you are! You want to rob me!"

He had fallen upon this crazy suspicion in his ramblings, and it gave him a peculiar delight to repeat it over and over. He leered shrewdly and cruelly as he said it, and the minister's heart broke within him. But his kindness did not leave him, nor his great love for the other helpless old man. . . .

The old sailor particularly delighted in shouting his insane charges when he felt people staring at him. . . . They would invariably cast suspicious eyes at the minister . . . and one or two strangers spoke reprovingly to him, and looking for a policeman, could not find him, and so did not interfere. . . .

And then the two old men, in their difficult passage of the rushing, noisy avenue, came again within the bold illumination of a saloon. Hordes moved before and around it, and its hot, strong breath came out in an assault upon the sweetness of the October wind. The old sailor's eyes kindled as he saw it, and he shook himself like a big dog in the grip of the other.

God Is Love

"I'm going in there," he muttered, struggling to be free. "Lemme alone."

"Brother—" the minister pleaded, holding as tightly as his strength let him.

"Lemme go! I want to go in there!"

"Brother, there is nothing in there for you," the old minister said.

"Lemme go, I tell ye! I want to go in and lick that bartender!"

"That's not the place," the minister cried. "Don't go in. Come home with me."

"Lemme alone, you thief, you! I'm not going with you, you thief!"

The old sailor tried to wrench himself from the other's grasp and was too successful, for he toppled into a bleary heap on the pavement. The minister bent over him sadly, and lifted him to his feet again. A little stunned, the sailor walked a few steps in a docile daze. Then the alcohol madness fell upon him again, and he began his muttering and struggle.

"Lemme go, you thief!" he said more violently than before. "LEMME GO!"

He gave a sudden shout, and made a great muscular twist which almost threw the minister to the ground.

"Thief! thief!" the old sailor shouted rabidly in his huge voice. One of his big whirling fists caught the feeble little minister square on the mouth, and the blood spat out. Sick and dizzy, the old minister clung to the other still, with the hope in his mind that the sailor would soon tire.

But the old sailor lashed himself into a greater

fury, as the blind fighting devils woke in his brain.

"Thief! thief!" and he mauled the other with great vicious blows, leaving marks wherever he struck. The two wrestled to the pavement, and black flowing waves of people turned aside from their usual channels along the avenue and foamed about them, as about the center of a whirlpool. There were wits in the crowd. One cried out above the dinning of the street noises, "Go it, you old roosters!" Another shouted, "My bet on the big guy," after the sailor had pounded his iron fist into the other's eye with a distinct crash. Everybody laughed at these witticisms; everyone in the crowd was in fine humor. The crowd spread and grew constantly, grew to sudden feverish immensity with curious men and boys, and pale, pitying or amused women. The antics and ridiculous contortions of the old men brought forth gales of laughter, cheers and hootings.

The little minister yielded to it all with a sick sorrow, taking the beating as he lay in the dirt without an ounce of resistance. He was too brokenhearted to fight, but shut his eyes and suffered each blow in silence, only groaning a little and weeping weakly through it all. . . . It was as if he did not care any more. . . .

The elevated stormed overhead, the street-cars clanked by, wagon wheels rattled, the peddlers barked hoarsely, the young girls still screamed joyously as they ran from pursuant lovers. Beyond the hanging dark, the sky watched as stonily as before. . . .

And a hurdy-gurdy rang out. The two old men thrashed about in the swill of the street, bruising themselves terribly. And the crowd stood about and sucked Olympian bliss out of the farce. Then a wide form in blue battered through the crowd and loomed over the two old men.

"A cop, a cop," rustled the crowd with respect. It hushed before authority, and in the silence could be heard the repeated cracks of the policeman's loaded club on the ribs of the old men. . . . He began hitting instantly. . . .

And soon the sailor collapsed, and lay limp on the limper form of the other. The policeman lifted both of them by the scruff of the neck and held their swaying forms steady with each of his big hands.

"You bastards, you!" he spat with loathing, as he regained his breath. . . . He hated them, for they had given him work to do. . . .

"You bastards!" . . . He hauled them to a telephone, and the old minister heard through a red daze the patrol wagon clattering up a few minutes later. He wondered what they would do with him, and did not care. . . . He felt hollow and dark within, and his body was a hammer that beat endlessly against itself. . . . He wept. . . .

And then they threw the two old men with "souls" into the depths of the van. And the crowd ebbed away grinning, chewing the happy cud of reminiscence.

The hardy old sailor slept as the wagon bounced over the cobblestones, snoring away all his aches and pains. But the old minister could do nothing but weep, holding his shredded face in his hands and weeping sorely.

One of the policemen pulled away his hands and asked, "What's the idea?" not unkindly.

But the old man did not answer, for he really did not know why he wept so terribly. He could only feel his agonized, welted body, and more terribly he could feel a queer void within him, from whence something had become uprooted. . . .

There was a recurring, overmastering, soul-shaking sense of desolation which came over him like a darkness, the feeling that Some One or Something had tricked him. . . . He wept and wept.

He wept as the sergeant at the desk took his name and charged him on the books with having been drunk and disorderly. He wept as he was led into the dark basement of the station house where the cells were.

In the sickly gaslight a keeper came forward rattling great keys. He had a bristling, round head, and narrow, cold eyes, and he stared at the two old men with hard and blasé impersonality.

"We're all filled up to-night, John," he said to the officer. "I guess we'll have to put these two in with that crazy Billy-Sunday nigger."

A cell was unlocked, and the old minister felt himself jammed into it by a single positive push of the keeper's hand. The sailor fell into a grotesque heap on the boards of the cell, and sprawled there, snoring almost immediately. But the other man leaned against the bars, his face in his hands, weeping.

He could do nothing but weep. There was no light in his brain; and he had lost all he had ever owned. He was alone at the bottom of a black sea of pain; alone. He sobbed and sobbed. And then through his pain he heard a singing and a muttering from the obscure part of the cell. He put his hands away and looked there, and saw strange, burning eyes. It was the insane Negro. In a shrill, unhuman and piercing strange voice he sang a hymn the minister had loved:

*"Abide with me, fast falls the eventide,
 The darkness deepens, Lord, with me abide—"*

The minister shuddered. He sobbed. He felt he could not suffer much more. "Hallelujah praise the Lord," burst out from the corner of the cell. Then the insane Negro again sang the hymn with its burden of trust and yearning and love of God:

*"When other helpers fail, and comforts flee,
 O Thou who changest not, abide with me."*

He sang it again with hysterical fervency. Chaos, despair, inextinguishable loneliness fell upon the old minister. . . . The disastrous, whirling sense of having been betrayed returned to him . . . the stifling void . . . the sense of having been betrayed by One he had loved.

"Abide with me, fast fall . . ."

The words twisted like inquisitorial screws into the brain of the old man. Their significance made him writhe. He could not bear this hurt any longer. It was as if the whole night had conspired to torture him. Something must snap. It was his soul which suddenly broke with a great shudder and spilled like poison through his blood. At the fifth time the Negro sang this hymn, the old minister gave out a great cry of madness. He flung himself fully and madly at the face and chest of the insane Negro.

"Don't, don't, don't, don't," he sobbed fiercely. But the Negro gave a queer scream like that of some night-prowling carnivore. He turned on the old minister and tore at him with teeth, claws and feet . . . hungrily. . . . Blood spurted on the dark cell air. . . . And nobody heard or came to rescue the gentle old man who had sought God all his days.

THE DAMNED AGITATOR

This textile strike was smoldering into its seventh week. It was a bitter ash in the mouths of the men. Funds were at an ebb, scabs were coming in like a locust plague, the company officials were growing more and more militant in their self-righteousness. The strikers were drifting into a state of depression and self-distrust. Their solidarity was beginning to show fissures and dangerous cracks.

All of which beat in with the morning light on Kurelovitch's tired brain. He lifted his head from the pillow, looked about the bleak bedroom, and heaved a long, weary, sigh.

At a meeting of company executives Kurelovitch had once been denounced as a dangerous agitator, whose pathological thirst for violence had created and sustained the strike.

"The man is a menace, a mad dog! His career ought to be stopped before he does any more mischief!" shouted one venerable director, his kindly blue eyes developing a glare that would have horrified the women folk of his family.

"The scoundrel's probably pocketing half the strike funds!" declared another director, his plump, rosy gills quivering, his bald head inflamed with rage, as he banged the table with his fist.

But Kurelovitch was not a mad dog. He was not waxing fat with industrial spoils, as had the directors. He was a tall, tragic, rough-hewn Pole, who had suddenly been hammered into leadership by the crisis of the strike. He had the burning eyes of a hungry worker, a rugged nose and mustaches, and his hands were ungainly and work-twisted. Yes, everything about him told a simple tale; this was a worker.

Now as he extricated himself from the bedclothes and sat up to dress, the strike problems writhed and hissed in his jaded brain, like a nest of snakes. For seven weeks now he had risen at dawn and had labored till midnight at this gigantic new task of winning a 15 per cent wage increase for his fellow workers. The simple worker had grown somber and wise in the process; skeptical of men and of words. He had seen plans collapse, heads broken unjustly, sentences inflicted by corrupt judges, babies and women starving. He had heard himself assailed as a monster by the other camp, and as a weakling and tool by the more embittered of his own side.

His wife had heard him sigh. She called from the kitchen, where she was moving about.

"No coffee for you this morning, Stanislaw," she announced in a sullen voice. "And there's nothin' else to eat, only a few hunks of old bread."

Kurelovitch stumbled wearily to his feet and entered the malodorous kitchen. Greasy pans and platters and sour garbage were scattered about, hopelessly, and in an opaque cloud of smoke his wife fussed over the stove, their fourth child kicking in her arms. She was heating a little milk for the infant, and when her husband entered, she turned on him with an amazing burst of wrath.

The Damned Agitator

"No, not a taste of food in the house!" she cried. "And the kids went to bed last night without any supper. I can't stand it!"

"But it's not my fault, now, is it, Annie?" the big man said humbly as he put his arm about her and the child. She cast it off fiercely, stood him off with a volley of words that were like poisoned arrows, each piercing to his vitals.

"It is your fault!" she screamed out of her overladen heart. "You were one of the first to go on strike, though we hadn't a penny in the house! Last week when the company wanted the men to come back you talked them out of it!"

"But, Annie—" the tall man attempted gently.

"Don't Annie me, or try to fool me with one of your speeches. You know the strike's lost as well as I do, and that after it you'll be blacklisted in every mill town in New England. But you don't care if your children starve, do you? You'd be glad to see us all dead, wouldn't you?"

The man crumpled under the attack; he seemed to grow smaller than his infuriated wife. Then he straightened in the gloom of the kitchen, and walked to the door.

"I'll try and get you a lot of groceries and things from headquarters this morning, Annie," he said in a husky voice, as he went out into the streets.

Kurelovitch shivered at his contact with the gray, sharp air. Snow had fallen during the night, but was now a noisome slush, after its brief experience with the mill town. The ooze squirmed through the gaps in his shoes, and started the gooseflesh along

Kurelovitch's spine. Across the river in the drab morning he could see the residential heights where the bosses lived. They reminded him of the village of his youth, with its girdle of snow-crowned hills and peaceful cottages. He remembered a Polish song of his youth, and shivered, then pulled himself together.

From the little bridge which bound the split halves of the town, he could see the mill, its shadows on the rotting ice of the river. The beautiful emblem of America gleamed from a staff on the low, sprawling structure, as if to sanctify all that went on beneath. And now Kurelovitch had traversed a jungle of decaying workers' shacks and offal-strewn streets, and was directly within the massive shadow of the mill. Two or three of his fellow-workers recognized him, and came hurrying forward from the picket line. Kurelovitch's day had begun.

"Them damned gunmen are sure out for fight this morning!" said a somber, chunky Pole, swathed in old burlap and a tremendous fur cap that had come with him from Europe.

"Yep, they licked up more booze than usual last night, I guess," said another striker between his chattering teeth.

A young picket burst out in a bitter voice, "Well, we'll give them all the fight they want, the bastards! We ain't yellow!" Kurelovitch looked at the young picket quietly, then the three pickets went with him to where fifty strikers walked slowly up and down the length of the mill gates.

The dark, silent men and women in the line seemed

like a host of mourners in this world of dreary sky and slush-laden earth. They were muffled to the chins, and their breaths rose like steam from human tea-kettles. A mood of sadness and suspense hung about the ragged mourners. Whenever they passed the knot of gunmen at the gate they turned their eyes away in grief.

Two of the gunmen, as if at a signal, detached themselves from the mob of them huddled at the gate. They carried clubs in their hands, and at their hips could be seen bulging the badges of their mission in life, which was to break strikes and to do murder.

They came close to Kurelovitch and watched him with sneering, sadistic eyes. As he walked up and down in the sluggish picket line, they dogged him and called him foul names. They were lusty and well-fed, these young athletes, and seemed to enjoy their work. Kurelovitch swallowed the lump in his throat.

An hour later, as he was departing from the line, the two gunmen still followed him. A group of pickets formed a guard about Kurelovitch and escorted him to the strike headquarters, shivering all the way with repressed rage. Kurelovitch was a marked man in the strike zone, and his maiming was a subject of much yearning and planning by the gunmen.

The daily meetings of the strikers were held in a great barn-like structure in the center of the tangled streets and alleys of the textile workers' slum. A burst of oratory smote Kurelovitch as he entered the great room, and a thousand faces, staring row on row, turned to the leader as he marched in.

"Kurelovitch, Kurelovitch has come!" ran a murmur like wind through a forest.

Kurelovitch leaped on the rough stage, where others of the strike committee were sitting, and whispered in consultation with a fellow Pole. He learned that there was nothing of moment that day—no sign from the bosses nor funds from sympathizers. It was merely another of the dark days of the strike.

"But some of the French-Canadians are getting shaky," the man whispered. "Rambeau has been at them, and yesterday their priest told them to go back to work. Give 'em hell, Kurelovitch!"

Kurelovitch came to the edge of the platform in a hush like that of an operating room, looking out over a foam of faces. They were faces that had blown into the golden land on the twelve winds of the world, dark Greek, and Latin faces, pale women's faces, the broad-boned, earthy, beautiful faces of Slavdom. Daylight struggled through large windows and dusted the heads and shoulders of the strikers as with a transcendent powder. An oilcloth sign behind Kurelovitch proclaimed in big, battering letters, "We Average $9 a Week and We Are Demanding 15 Per Cent More! Are You With Us?"

The air tightened as Kurelovitch loomed there, this sad proletarian hero, stooped and gaunt with his many cares. Finger-deep hollows were in his cheeks, and, with his blazing eyes and strong mouth, he seemed like some ascetic follower of the warrior Mohammed.

"Fellow workers . . ."

In a low voice he began discussing the secular

details of the strike, as on every day. It was drab and yet dramatic; this talk of food, arrests, injunction. Then something would come over Kurelovitch, a strange feeling of automatism, as if he were indeed the voice that this simple-hearted horde had created out of their woe. The searing phrases rushed from his lips in a wild, stormy music, like the voice of a gale, and as mystic and powerful.

With both hands holding his breast, as if it were bursting with passionate vision, Kurelovitch lifted his face in one of the superb moments that had made him a leader.

"Fellow workers!" he chanted, rising to his symphonic climax, "we can never be beaten, for we are the workers on whose shoulders rest the pillars of the world! In our hands are the tools by which life is carried on!

"We are beginning to starve, some of us, but let us starve bravely, for we are soldiers in a greater and nobler war than that which is bleeding Europe. We are soldiers in the class war which is finally to set mankind free of all war and all poverty, all bosses and hate. Workingmen of the world, unite; we have nothing to lose but our chains; we have a world to gain!"

Kurelovitch ended in a great shout, and then the handclapping and whistles rose to him in turbulent swirls. He found himself suddenly weary and limp and melancholy, and his deepest wish was to go off somewhere alone to wait until the hollow places inside were refilled. . . .

But, with the others of the strike committee, he

left the platform and fused into the discussions that were raging everywhere. Everybody tried to come near Kurelovitch, to speak to him. He was a common hearth at which his people crowded and shouldered for warmth, his starving, hopeful people who believed him when he said they could wipe out the accumulated woe of humanity. . . .

He was treated to long recitals of the workings of the proletarian soul in this time of want and panic and anger. He heard a hundred tales of temptation, of desperate hunger, of outrages at the hands of gunmen. Kurelovitch listened to it all like a grave, kind father, untying many a Gordian knot with his new-found strength and understanding.

And then came to him Rambeau, the leader of the French-Canadians, a short, black, wrinkled man, with slow eyes that became living coals of fire when passion breathed on them.

He was angry to impotence now. "You said in your speech that I was a traitor, Kurelovitch," he shouted fiercely. "You lie; I am not. But we others think this strike is lost, and that we'd all better go back before it's too late."

"It's not lost," Kurelovitch replied slowly. "The mills can't work full time until we choose to go back. And, Rambeau, I say again that you're a scab and traitor if you go back now."

Rambeau flushed purple with wrath, and rushed upon the tall Pole as if to devour him. But Kurelovitch did not lift his stern, calm gaze from the other's face, and a light like that of bayonets came and went in his blue eyes. The two touched, chest to chest; it looked like a fight, but then Kurelovitch intrigued the other into a sensible discussion that served to keep the French-Canadians on the firing line. . . .

And so it went. So Kurelovitch passed his day, moving from the brink of one crisis to another. He sat with the strike committee for many hours in a smoky room and agonized over ways and means. He addressed another large meeting at headquarters in the afternoon. He went on the picket line again, and was again singled out for threats and taunts by the gunmen, so that he felt murder boiling up inside him, and left. Then he had to return later to the picket line because word came that five of the pickets had been arrested in a fight finally precipitated by the gunmen. Kurelovitch spent the rest of the afternoon scurrying about and finding bail for the five.

Toward night he had a supper of ham sandwiches and coffee. Then he and three of the strike committee went to a meeting of sympathizers in another industrial town fifteen miles away. Kurelovitch made his third impassioned speech of the day, and stirred up a large collection. The long, dull, wrenching ride home followed.

He got off the trolley car near his house about midnight, his brain whirling and hot, his heart despairing. The urgency of the fight was passed, and nothing was left to buoy him against his weariness. He walked in a stupor; the day had sucked every atom of his valor and strength.

There was a light waning and wavering in the window of his little three-room flat. He was surprised at this, for the hour was late. When he had fumbled with the lock and opened the door he was amazed to see his wife sitting near the stove. She stood up and turned on him like a wild beast in its cave.

"You dirty dog!" she screamed at Kurelovitch in the quiet night. "You swine!"

"Annie, dear—"

"To go away in the morning and leave us to starve! To send food to others' families and then to forget us! Oh, you'd be glad if we all died of starvation! You'd laugh to see us all dead, you murderer!"

Kurelovitch was too sad to attempt any answer. He went to the bedroom where he and two of the children slept and shut the door behind him. His wife took this for a gesture of contempt, and her frenzy mounted to a blood-curdling crescendo that ran up and down the neighborhood. Heads popped out of windows and bawled to her to shut up for Christ's sake. And, finally she broke down of sheer exhaustion and Kurelovitch heard her shuffling into bed.

There was anguished silence, and then Kurelovitch heard his poor drudge of a wife weeping, with gulping sobs that hurt him like knives. . . .

And now he could not sleep at all, even after her sobbing had merged into ugly snoring. He tossed as in a fever, as he had on so many other nights of the seven frantic weeks of the strike.

He got up and stumbled to the window, and looked out at the cold night. The shabby slum street dwindled to a line, the mass of the mill building could be seen dominating over the houses. No one was abroad in the dark; he saw a chain of lanterns casting morbid shadows, and the wind whipping up the litter of the streets. All was icy, desolate and inimical. The stars were white and high overhead, as distant as hope from the place where Kurelovitch burned with sleeplessness. He heard the sordid snoring of his wife.

He ached with a great need for escape. As he twitched on his bed the days that had gone and the darker days to come leaped around him and taunted him like fiends. The feeling that on him the fate of the strike rested made him sweat with terror. His starving children made him gasp, and writhe.

He must forget. There was no hope anywhere. He groped his way to a little dresser in the room. He found a bottle there. He took it to bed with him, and drank, and drank again, till the past and the future were blurred in one and the great wings of peace folded over him and he sank into the maternal arms.

On the morrow he would wake and find the ring of strike problems haunting him again. He would grapple with them again in his big, tragic fashion. Thus he would go on and on till he was broken or dead, for Kurelovitch had dared to spit into the face of the beast that reigns over mankind. He had sinned; he was truly a damned agitator. But drunk and tortured and cowardly or brave, he must go on, and others would follow him. A new world was being born out of his agonies.

THE PASSWORD TO THOUGHT—
TO CULTURE

The factory of Fineberg and Goldstone, Makers of the Hytone Brand Ladies' Cloaks and Suits, rushed along busily in its usual channels that sweet May afternoon; the machines racing and roaring; the workers gripped by their tasks; the whole dark loft filled with a furious mechanical life, hot and throbbing as the pulse of an airplane.

Outside, the sunlight lay in bright patterns on the dusty streets and buildings, illuminating for another two hours the city crowds moving to and fro on their ever-mysterious errands. But the factory was filling with darkness, and the hundred silent figures at the sewing machines bent even lower to their work, as if there were some mighty matter for study before them, needing a sterner and tenser notice as the day deepened into twilight.

The pressers, at their boards at one end of the long loft, thumped with their irons, and surrounded themselves with hissing steam like a fog. The motors roared and screamed, and one of the basters, a little Italian girl, sang in a high voice a sad, beautiful love song of her native province in Italy. It ran through the confusion of the loft like a trickle of silver, but now and again its fragile beauty was drowned by the larger, prosaic voice of Mr. Goldstone, the junior partner, as he bustled about and shouted commands to one or another of his workers.

"Chaim, come here and take this bundle to Abe's machine!" he would shout in Yiddish, and a very old, white-bearded Jew came patiently and slowly, and took the huge bundle of cloaks on his brittle shoulders, and delivered them to the operator.

"Hurry up on this Flachsman job, boys!" Mr. Goldstone would say, rubbing his hands, as he stood behind one of the operators, and a few of them in the vicinity would frown slightly and murmur some inaudible answer from between closed lips.

Mr. Goldstone, a short, flabby man with a bald head and reddish mustache that was turning white, was the practical tailor of the firm and stayed in the factory and looked after production. His partner had been a salesman when they joined their poverty and ambition not many years ago, and therefore looked after the selling and business end now. Mr. Goldstone liked this arrangement, for he had sat at the bench for years, and still liked the smell of steam and the feel of cloth, the putting together of "garments." Best of all, he liked to run things, to manage, to bustle, and to have other tailors under him, dependent on his word.

He trudged about the factory all day like a minor Napoleon, and wherever he went there was a tightening of nerves, an increased activity of fingers, and a sullenness as if his every word were an insult. He was a good manager, and kept things moving. His very presence was like a lash lightly flicked at the backs of the workers. They did not like him, but they responded when they felt him near.

Mr. Goldstone trotted about more strenuously than usual on this afternoon. There was a big order to be delivered the next morning, and he was making sure that it would be on time. He sped from his basters to his pressers, from his pressers to his operators, a black, unlighted cigar in his mouth, a flush of worry on his gross, round face.

"Where are those fifty suits in the 36 size of the Flachsman lot?" he suddenly demanded of the white-bearded factory porter.

"I brought them to David an hour ago, Mr. Goldstone," Chaim said, looking at him with meek eye.

"Good. Then they'll be sure to get off to-night," said the Boss, scowling like a busy general. "Good."

He thought a moment, and then hurried on his short legs through the piles of unfinished clothing till he came to the door that led from the factory to the shipping room. There was a glass panel in the upper part of the door, and Mr. Goldstone stopped and looked through it before entering.

What he saw made him take the cigar out of his mouth, swear, and then open the door with a violent kick that almost tore it from its hinges.

"My God!" he cried fervently, "what is this, anyways?"

His shipping clerk, David Brandt, a Jewish youth of about twenty-one, was seated on the table near the open window, staring dreamily at the gray masses of building opposite, that now were flashing with a thousand fires in the sun. He was hugging his knees, and beside him on the table lay an open green-

The Password To Thought—To Culture 47

covered book that he had evidently put aside for a moment.

David Brandt was a well-built youth, with good shoulders and chest, a body that would have been handsome had he not carried it like a sloven; tense brown eyes, and a lean face with hungry, high Slavic features. He was shabbily dressed, almost downright dirty in his carelessness of shirt and clothes, and he stood up hastily as the Boss spoke and ran his fingers nervously through a shock of wild black hair.

Mr. Goldstone strode over to him, picked up the book, and read the title.

"Ruskin's Sea-same and Lilies!" he pronounced contemptuously. "My God, boy, is this what we're payin' you good money for? What are you here for anyway, to work or to stuff yourself with fairy tales? Tell me!" he demanded.

"To work," David answered reluctantly, his eyes fixed on the floor.

"Then work, in God's name, work! This ain't a public library, ye know, or a city college for young shipping clerks to come to for a free education! What sort of a book is this, anyway?" he asked staring again at the title. "What's a sea-same, anyway?"

"It's a sort of password," David stammered, a crimson wave of blood creeping over his dark face.

"A password to what?" the Boss demanded, looking at him sternly, with the air of a judge determined upon the whole truth and nothing but the truth. "Is it something like the Free Masons?"

David floundered guiltily. "It's used only in a

sort of symbolical sense here," he explained. "Seasame was used as a password by Ali Baba in the story, when he wanted to get into the robbers' cave, but here it means the password to thought—to culture."

"To thought—to culture!" Mr. Goldstone mimicked grandiosely, putting an imaginary monocle to his eye, and walking a few mincing steps up and down the room. "And I suppose, Mr. Brandt, while you was learning the password to Thought and to Culture—ahem!"—he put an incredible sneer into these two unfortunate words—"you forgot all about such little things like that Flachsman lot! Look at it, it's still laying around, and Chaim brought it in an hour ago! My God, boy, this can't go on, ye know! I been watching you for the past two months, and I'll tell you frankly, you ain't got your mind on business! I didn't know what it was before, but I see now it's this Thought"—he sneered again—"and this Culture. Cut it out, see? If ye want to read, do it outside the factory, and read something that'll bring you in dividends—good American reading."

"Yes."

"What do ye want with thought and culture, anyway?" the Boss cried, waving his cigar like an orator. "Me and Mr. Fineberg was worse off than you once; we started from the bottom; and look where we got to without sea-sames *or* lilies! You're wasting your good time, boy."

David looked at the plump little Jew, with his glittering bald head, his flabby face, and his perfectly rounded stomach that was like some fleshly

The Password To Thought—To Culture 49

monument to years of champagne suppers, auto rides, chorus girl debauches, and all the other splendid rewards of success in the New York garment trade.

"Do you ever read Shakespeare?" Mr. Goldstone said more tolerantly, as he lit his cigar.

"Yes."

"Well, you know in his Choolyus Cæsar, this man Cæsar says: Let me have men about me that are fat, and that don't think; that is, don't think outside of business, ye understand. Well, that's my advice to you, my boy, especially if ye want to hold your job and got any ambition. The last feller that held your job was made a salesman on the road after five years, and the same chances are open to you. Now let's see whether you're smart or not. I like you personally, but you gotta change your ways. Now let's see you use common sense after this—not Thought and Culture."

He laughed a broad, gurgling, self-satisfied laugh, and passed into the factory again, where the machines were warring, and the little Italian girl singing, and the pressers were sending up their strange, white fog of steam.

David spat viciously at the door that closed behind him.

2.

He worked fiercely all that afternoon, in a state of trembling indignation; his hands shook, and his forehead perspired with the heat of the internal fires that consumed him. He was debating over and over again the problem of thought and culture with Mr. Goldstone, and his eyes would flash as he made some striking and noble point, and withered the fat little Boss with his scorn.

Six o'clock came at last; the factory motors were shut off, and died away with a last lingering scream. The operators and pressers and basters became men and women again. They rose stiffly from their seats, and talked and laughed, and dressed themselves and hurried away from the factory as from a prison.

The rage that sustained David died with the iron-throated wailing of the whistles that floated over the city, unyoking so many thousands of weary shoulders.

A curious haze came upon him then. He walked home weakly, as if in a debilitating dream. He hardly felt the scarlet sky above the roofs, the twilight beginning to fall upon the city like a purple doom, the air rich with spring. Mighty streams were flowing through the factory district, human working masses silent and preoccupied after the day's duties, and David slipped into these broad currents without thought, and followed them automatically.

He lived in a tenement on Forsythe Street, on the East Side, and the tides all flowed in that direction; down Broadway, through Grand Street and Prince Street and other streets running east and west and across the dark, bellowing Bowery. Then they spread again and filtered and poured out into the myriad criss-crossing streets where stand the tenements row after row, like numberless barracks built for the conscripts of labor.

It was Friday night, the eve of the East Side's Sabbath, and Mrs. Brandt, David's little, dark, round-backed mother, was blessing the candles when he entered. She had a white kerchief over her hair, and her brown eyes, youthful and eager in her wrinkled face as David's own, shone with a pious joy as she read the pre-Sabbath ritual from an old *Sidar* that had come with her from Russia. She looked at David's clouded face anxiously for a moment, but did not interrupt her prayers to greet him when he came in. David did not greet her either, but limp and nerveless went directly to his room and flung himself upon the bed.

There he lay for a few minutes in the darkness. He heard the sounds of life rising from the many windows on the air-shaft; the clatter of dishes and knives, the crying of babies, voices lifted in talk. He heard his mother move about; she had evidently finished her prayers, and was coming to his room. Some strange weakness suddenly assailed him; as she knocked at the door, David began weeping; quietly, reasonlessly, like a lonely child.

"David?" his mother inquired, waiting at the threshold. There was no answer, and she called his name again.

"David!"

David answered this time.

"I'm all right, Mommer," he said, his voice muffled by the pillow.

"Supper'll be ready in five or ten minutes," Mrs. Brandt said. "Better come out now and wash yourself. And David—"

"Yes?"

"David, darling," she whispered, opening the door a little, "you should not do like you did to-night. You should always go and kiss your Popper the first thing when you come home. You don't know how bad it makes him feel when you don't do that. He cries over it, and it makes him sicker. He's very sick now; the doctor said to-day your Popper is worse than he's ever seen him. Be a good boy, David, go and speak to him."

"Yes, Mommer," David said wearily, "after supper."

He washed at the sink, and ate the Friday night supper of stuffed fish, noodle soup, boiled chicken and tea. His mother chattered to him all the while, but David listened in that haze that had come on him at the end of the factory day, and answered her vaguely. When he had finished eating he continued sitting at the supper table, and was only aroused when she again suggested that he go in to see his father.

The elder Brandt was a sad, pale, wasted little Jew who had spent fourteen years in the sweatshops of America, and now, at the age of forty-five, was ready to die.

He had entered the factories a hopeful immigrant, with youthful, rosy cheeks that he had brought from Russia, and a marvelous faith in the miracle of the Promised Land that had come from there, too. The sweatshops had soon robbed him of that youthful bloom, however; then they had eaten slowly, like a beast in a cave gnawing for days at a carcass, his

The Password To Thought—To Culture

lungs, his stomach, his heart, all his vital organs, one by one.

The doctor came to see him twice a week, and wondered each time how he managed to live on. He lay in the bed, propped up high against the pillows, a Yiddish newspaper clutched in his weary hand. His face, wax-yellow and transparent with disease, was the face of a humble Jewish worker, mild and suffering, but altogether dead now except for the two feverish eyes. He put down the newspaper and looked up with a timid smile as David entered the room. David came over and kissed him, and then sat on a chair beside his father's bed.

"Well, David, boy, did you have a hard day in the shop to-day?" the sick man began in a weak voice, fingering his straggly beard and trying to appear cheerful.

"Yes," David answered dully.

"Are you getting on good there?" Mr. Brandt continued, in his poor, hopeful quaver.

"Yes."

"And did you ask the boss yet about that raise he promised you two months ago?"

"No," said David, vacantly, staring with lusterless eyes at the floor.

Mr. Brandt looked apprehensive, as if he had made an error in asking the question. He stroked the feather-bed quilt under which he lay imprisoned, and stole little anxious glances at David's brooding face, as if to implore it for the tiniest bit of attention and pity. Another difficult question hesitated on his lips.

"David, dear," he said at last, "why don't you come in to see your Popper any more when you get home from work?"

"It's because I'm tired, I guess," David answered.

"No; it ain't that, Davidka. You know it ain't. You used to come in regular and tell me all the news. Do you hate your Popper now, David?"

"No; why should I?"

"I don't know. God knows I've done all I could for you; I worked night and day for long years in the shop, thinking only of you, of my little son. I wanted better things for you than what you've got, but I couldn't help myself; I was always only a workingman. Some men have luck; and they are able to give their children college educations and such things. But I've always been a *shlemozel;* but you must try to get more out of life than I have found."

"Yes."

"David, don't hate me so; you hardly want to speak to me. Look at me."

David turned his eyes toward his father, but he saw him only dimly, and heard in the same dim way the feeble, high voice uttering the familiar lamentations. In the flickering gaslight his father seemed like some ghostly shadow in a dream.

"David, you hate me because I'm sick and you have to support me along with your mother. I know; I know! Don't think I don't see it all! But it's not my fault, is it, Davie, and I've only been sick a year, and who knows, maybe soon I will be able to take my place in the shop again, and earn my own bread, as I did for so many years before."

"Don't, Popper, for God's sake, don't talk about it!" David spoke sharply.

"All right, I won't. All right. Excuse me."

They sat in silence, and then David moved uneasily, as if to go. Mr. Brandt reached over and took his hand in his own moist, trembling one, and held it there.

"Davie," he said, "Davie, dear, tell me why you didn't come in to see me to-night. I must know."

"I was tired, Popper, I told you."

"But why were you tired?"

"I had a fight in the shop."

"A fight? With whom?"

"With the boss—with Mr. Goldstone."

"With the boss? God in heaven, are you crazy? Are you going to lose your job again? What is wrong with you? You have never stuck to one job more than six months. Can't you do like other boys, and stick to a job and make a man of yourself?"

"Let me alone!" David cried in sudden rage, rushing from the room. "For God's sake, let me alone!"

3.

With both elbows on the sill, and with his face in his hands, David sat at the airshaft window again during the next half-hour. His mind whirled with formless ideas, like the rout of autumn leaves before a wind. His head throbbed, and again a haze had fallen upon him, a stupor painful as that of a man with a great wound.

The airshaft was still clamorous with the hymn of life that filled it night and day. Babies were squalling, women were berating their children, men were talking in rapid Yiddish, there was rattling of plates and knives, and the shrieking of the clothes line pulley like a knife through it all. The airshaft was dark; and overhead, in the little patch of sky, three stars shone down. Pungent spring odors mingled with the smell of rubbish in the courtyard below.

David's mother moved about carefully as she took away the supper dishes. She knew David's moods, and went on tiptoe, and let him sit there until she had cleaned up in the kitchen. He heard vaguely the sound of her labors, and then she came and laid her rough hand, still red and damp from the dish-water, on his shoulder.

"What's the matter, Davie?" she asked, tenderly. "What are you worrying about?"

"Nothing."

"Why did you fight with your Popper? You know he's sick, and that you mustn't mind what he says. Why did you do it?"

"I don't know."

"You must be nice to him now; he feels it terribly because he's sick, and that you have to support him. Do you worry because you have to support us?"

"I don't know."

"It won't last forever, Davie boy. Something must happen—there must come a change. God can't be so bad as all that. Is that what worries you?"

The Password To Thought—To Culture 57

David's eyes grew melancholy and his head sunk more deeply between his hands.

"Life isn't worth living; that's what's the trouble, Mommer," he said. "I feel empty and black inside, and I've got nothing to live for."

"That's foolishness," his mother said warmly. "Every one lives, and most people have even more troubles than us. If there are so many poor, we can be poor, too. What do you think God put us here for anyway? A healthy young boy like you saying he's got nothing to live for! It's a disgrace!"

"Mommer," David said, passionately, "can you tell me why you live? Why do you yourself live? Give me one good reason!"

"Me? Are you asking me this question?" David's mother exclaimed, in a voice in which there was surprise mixed with a certain delight that her usually silent boy was admitting her on an equality to such intimacies.

She wrinkled her brow. It was the first time, probably, in her work-bound, busy life that she had thought on such a theme, and she put her finger on her lip in a characteristic gesture and meditated for a minute.

"Well, Davie," she said slowly, "I will tell you why your Popper and I have gone on struggling and living. It is because we loved you, and because we wanted to see you grow up healthy and strong and happy, with a family of your own around you in your old age. That's the real reason."

"But supposing I don't want to grow up," David cried. "Supposing you raised a failure in me—supposing I'm sick of this world—supposing I die before I raise a family—"

"That's all foolishness. Don't talk that way."

"But supposing—"

"I won't suppose anything."

"Very well," said David. "You live for me. But tell me, Mommer, what about people who have no children to live for? What does the whole human race live for? Do you know? Who knows any one that knows?"

Mrs. Brandt thought again. Then she dismissed the whole subject with a wave of her hand.

"Those are just foolish questions, like a child's," she said. "They remind me of the time when you were a little boy, and cried for days because I would not buy you an automobile, or a lion we saw in the Central Park, or some such thing. Why should we have to know why we live? We live because we live, Davie dear. You will have to learn that some day, and not from books, either. I don't know what's the matter with those books, anyway; they make you sick, Davie."

"No; it's life makes me sick—this dirty East Side life!"

"You're a fool! You must stop reading books, and you must stop sitting here every night, like an old graybeard. You must go out more and enjoy yourself."

"I have no friends."

"Make them! What a funny, changeable boy you are! Two or three years ago we could never keep you at home nights, you were so wild. You did nothing but go about till early morning with your friends—and fine friends they were too, pool-room loafers, gamblers, pimps, all the East Side filth. Now you read those library books; and I don't know which is worse. Go out; put on your hat and coat and go!"

"Where?"

"Anywhere! The East Side is big, and lots of things are going on! Find them!"

"But I want to read!"

"You won't! I won't let you! I should drop dead if I let you!"

David stared wrathfully at her for a moment, stung into anger by her presumptuous meddling into affairs beyond her world of illiteracy and hope. He was about to speak sharply to her, but changed his mind with a weary shrug of his shoulders. He put on his hat and coat and wandered aimlessly into the East Side night, to walk, to dream, to be surrounded by a million struggling Jews, and to be lonely in their midst.

THE AMERICAN FAMINE

(November, 1921)

There is a famine in Soviet Russia. There is a famine in fat America, too.

I have gone around New York these past few days, to see famine, to see the patient, ignorant men whom the rich are killing and taming in this periodical Spartan massacre of the helots.

One morning I stood before a bread-line on the Bowery. The dawn had just forced its way through the breach of sullen sky. There was a faint light in the city like that on sunken ships. The houses were stern, charred remnants against the sky; they smoldered in gloom. The elevated roared; Caliban rushing on the errands of man. All was old and bitter. Thousands of men and women, half-asleep, bloodless, shuffled on their way to the factories. Wagons rattled by. It was my tall, cruel city.

Before a mission of Jesus Christ, who died for Brotherhood, as Keats died for Beauty, as Liebknecht died that there might be Bread and Peace in the world, three hundred men stood shivering in line.

They had waited for hours in the dark and cold. They were soon to be rewarded with coffee and stale crullers.

Who were they? Who make up the unemployed? Workers. Workers: three giant American lumberjacks from the Maine woods, standing proudly and somberly like dying trees. Sailors, in rough, wrinkled clothes. Battered, emaciated factory hands. Dazed old derelicts with white, unshaven chins and doggish eyes. Young huskies, veterans of the war, usually slangy and cheerful, but hanging their heads in shame. Stokers, cooks, waiters, mechanics, farmers, drivers, clerks and longshoremen, useful citizens of the world, creators of wealth, the hard-handed architects of society. Unemployed. Hungry.

No one spoke. They stood there with hands thrust deep in pockets, braced against the wind. It was not necessary to say anything, one to the other. Each understood the other's shame. I, too, felt ashamed, as I stood and watched. I had five dollars in my pockets, besides the certainty of another month's living.

These men had nothing. Nothing!

The Bowery is a little city of the damned. It is the bottom of the whirlpool that sucks forever downward the frail boat of the wage worker. Here men come when they have made a misstep to one side or the other in the eternal tight-rope balancing over the precipice of hunger that is the proletarian life. Here they come when they are weakest, to seek Lethe in drink and dirt and shiftlessness. Here workers come when they are sick and friendless, and need a quiet place to die.

There are 600,000 men out of work in the imperial city of New York, 75,000 of whom are veterans of the late war for democracy, the Wilsonian liberal war for freedom, life, homes, wives, children, music, laughter, recreation, health, friendship—and jobs. These veterans on the bread line WON that war!

The Bowery is always full of homeless wanderers, but now it is overpopulated. The unemployed swarm on every street corner, in all the missions and lousy lodging-houses. It is a city of war refugees. I went into one of the Bowery missions that are scattered so freely under the loud elevated structure. These missions are the places where the rich preach humility to the poor. In the long, bare room, an overflow of men sat sleeping at a table meant for reading religious tracts. In a few hours they would be turned out into the night. A cheap altar stood in one corner, and over the reading table was hung an American flag. A hundred men in working clothes and overalls, silent and morbid. No one spoke—there is nothing to say when men are hungry. They sat and waited.

No watchful priest or attendant was about, so a drunken man had wandered in. He staggered about, a thick-set Swede with a raw, red face and blue, wondering childish eyes. He offered every one a drink of rot gut from a quart bottle. No one would take it. No one would joke with him, or answer him.

"Aw, c'm on, less all be happy," he pleaded. "C'm on, fellas, less be happy!" At last one man took a drink. The others were afraid they might be caught and put out.

Around Cooper Union, where the Bowery splits

off into Fourth avenue, the unemployed sit on the sleety benches under the shadow of the statue of Peter Cooper, who invented some marvelous machine or other that has reduced the burden of labor. They sit there every day and every night. They rarely speak. They sit and wait. They read old newspapers, and watch the busy people go by. They dream of nothing—they are hungry. They sit and wait.

There is the Bowery Y.M.C.A., a massive redbrick structure with hundreds of rooms and beds for those who have jobs and can pay. The unemployed flock here, too—we saw hundreds of them one night watching the free moving pictures that are provided for the starving. A handsome young bank president fights on the screen a villainous Wall Street broker for the hand of the most beautifully enameled heroine in the world. Ah, what a theme for the downcast hearts of starving men—what a banquet of Christian comfort and joy! There was a big bulletin board in the lobby, with a bold legend chalked on it: "GOD FORGIVES AND FORGETS—WHY NOT YOU?"

A dapper little Y.M.C.A. superintendent came up to me, as I was reading this masterpiece of the Christian brain.

"Ah, you don't look like a bum!" he said with the ready professional smile, and he offered to shake my hand, but I turned away.

Forgive and forget!

It rained the next morning as I set out; the city lay wrapped in gray smoke and rain. The faces of the houses were wet, the pavements were slimy as an eel, there was a chill wind. The damp penetrated through the paper shoes of the homeless thousands, the wind cut through their rags. Along the Bowery one saw knots of men flattened against the walls of the damp buildings, or cowering in doorways. They were still speechless.

About Cooper Square they had abandoned the benches and stood in doorways or under the entrance to the Cooper Union library. They were in the reading room, too, scores of them, grazing like slow-witted kine through the endless pages of the meadow-wide newspapers. They were not really reading, they were thinking of the coming night, when they would have to go out to find a bed.

I next went to the Grand Central railroad station where the American Land Brigade has established a farm employment bureau for ex-service men. Some four hundred men have applied here daily for jobs, the papers say, but only thirty and forty a day get them. The bureau occupies a great marble corridor on the west side of the station, a gigantic balcony overlooking the shuffle, the chaos, the movement and splendid excitement of the main floor of the station.

Hundreds of young men were here, all with the bronze service button in their lapels, many with the silver button that tells of heroic wounds. These were the boys who had been martyred for Wilson's ideals. These were the boys who had been roasted in a hell hotter than the insane creation imagined by the Christian priesthood. These were the boys who had shed blood for freedom. Now they stood

The American Famine

about in beggar's rags, hungry and jobless, with the dumb, animal look that now one sees everywhere in these faces. The nation that sainted them, that demanded the "supreme sacrifice" of them, now turns them off like mongrel dogs.

Scores of them were lying on the bare marble floor, sleeping in all the clamor of a great railroad terminal. Others squatted about on their haunches, miserably conversing. Above them and around them loomed the huge, wonderful monument of American industrialism. The superb arch of ceiling, a blue sky dotted with golden stars. The Romanesque square columns, tall as mountains, the marble floors and walls and balustrades. Luxury unbounded. It was a fitting frame to their misery, this ostentation. It was American shallowness, putting all its ardor and idealism into steel and stone, and letting men decay. It was American hypocrisy, a gorgeous body in which beat a putrid and inhuman heart. At ten o'clock every night these veterans were put out of the marble corridor, and they too must find the hunk of bread and the sleeping place somehow in the immense unfriendly city.

Scores of other ex-service men make a dwelling place these days of Bryant Park, which is a green square next to the Public Library at Fifth avenue and Forty-second street. Hundreds of the unemployed have made this park their rendezvous. The place is jammed with hungry, idle men every day, sprawling over the benches, sleeping on the grass, moving up and down the walks in close companionship like sheep in a storm. They have formed some sort of spontaneous organization here, and have their own law-and-order committee and other committees. Charitable men and women come here and distribute sandwiches and clothing occasionally, and Ledoux, the theosophist humanitarian, held some meetings with them. Twice the men were clubbed by the police, because they are out of jobs.

The cold, lustral rain had driven all the men out of the park on this day into doorways and other shelters. Twenty of them were jammed as tightly as human beings can be jammed into a little army recruiting tent on the grass. Five or six of them shivered under a beautiful marble fountain, and a group huddled under a statue of William Cullen Bryant, poet of Calm and Serenity. In the library reading rooms one found dozens of others, prowling about disconsolately, too distracted to read. The rain fell for another two hours. I read a book. When I came out of the library the sun was shining again. A hundred men were again promenading up and down the walks, for the grass and benches were wet and it was too cold to be sitting.

A group of unemployed had gathered about a little runt of a Jew, a five-foot hobo without a collar, who had a droll, wise, shrewd face like a gargoyle's, and the most mischievous little brown eyes. The men loved him, he was their fun-maker and jester. They buffeted him about, they kicked him and slapped him affectionately, and he laughed and dodged their rough blows.

"Come on, Shorty, make us a speech!" they cried.

"G'wan, I ain't the Mayor!"

"Come on, ye gotta, Shorty! Give us a speech!"

They stood him on a bench, and he grinned like a satyr, and put his hand in his old dusty coat, like a statesman.

"Ahem!" he began pompously, and the crowd rocked with glee.

Other men came running up for the fun. Some one produced a long false beard that had been gotten God-knows-where. Another man stuck his derby hat on Shorty, and a clean, middle-aged man, who looked like a respectable clerk, took out his precious glasses from their case and lent them to Shorty.

How they roared as they saw their favorite in this wonderful make-up! They could not contain their laughter; they slapped each other on the backs, and the tears came to their eyes.

"Give us a speech, Shorty!" they shouted.

"Gen'l'men," Shorty began, lifting a dirty hand, "attenshin. I'm goin' to undress you all on a great subjec'. Lissen: I'm a Bullshevik, and I want ye all to vote for me, see?"

"Hooray!" the crowd of jobless men shouted.

"I'm goin' tuh speak on unemployments," said Shorty sagely. "You know what that woid means, donchyer? It means bein' a millionaire without any money, see? Well, I just come back from Washington, boys, where I seen our President Harding. He wuz playin' gol-luf on his front lawn when I come up to see him, and when I told him I come from the Bryant Park boys he says he's too busy; he's only got time to see the boys from Fift' avenue. But then, when he found out that he used to buy his chewin'-

tobacco from a rich uncle of mine that runs a tobacco store in Marion, Ohio, he seen me, 'cause he knew I wuz honest.

"I told him about the unemployments, and he lissened to me nicely. Then I seen he wuz crying. He says to me, 'Lissen, Shorty, gee, I'm sorry to see you're hangin' out with that Bryant Park bunch! They're a bad lot, and they'll spoil ye, Shorty. Ye're too good for them bums—"

Here the crowd hauled Shorty down with a great whoop and pummeled him amid uncontrolled laughter. Shorty dodged about like a cat; he came up on his feet every time; nothing would ever keep Shorty down for long. He was the perfect city gamin, and he was in his element here. They set him up on the bench again. He took out a few frayed green cigar store coupons and held them up between his fingers.

"Some kind gen'l'men has just given me a hundred dollars for the boys out of work," he said with a big grin. "Who'll give me another hundred?"

He read several telegrams from an old yellow pad some one handed up to him.

"Bryant Park Committee—Send a hundred boys over to Blake's restaurant for supper. Tell them to walk quietly by twos and threes and make no noise. We don't like noise, especially the way they eat soup.
    (Signed)   THE HOLY ROLLERS."

There were loud ironic cheers.

"Another telegram, gen'l'men," Shorty announced importantly.

"Bryant Park Committee—Send two hundred fellers over here for a job Monday morning—seven o'clock—at the penitentiary.

(Signed)   THE BOARD OF HEALTH."

"Yes, gen'l'men, they're doin' everything they can for us. They all got kind hearts, and some day they're goin' to give us the earth, yes, they are. An' I'm goin' to be President some day, and I'll give ye all jobs, and we'll have gol-luf parties on the White House lawn, yes, we will."

It was just fooling; it was the unconscious wisdom of the proletariat, that waits for its proper time to burst all the shells and shams; it was Gavroche predicting the tumbrils, and they understood him, these men, though he did not know all he was saying, nor did they. The grim jests of the proletariat have tumbled down many a throne!

Some one said to me the other night:

"But how *do* these men live?"

I don't know; they live somehow; and many of them die.

I was coming through Union Square one night. A young fellow stepped out of a doorway and asked me for a cigarette. I gave it to him, and a few nickels. Then I talked with him. He was a young, clean-looking chap, with a lean American face, and blue, friendly eyes. Just the ordinary good-natured American boy who wears overalls.

"God, I don't know how this'll end for me. I've been out of work four months now, would you believe it? Haven't eaten for two days: I can't believe it yet. I can ask for a cigarette, but haven't got the nerve to ask for money. The cops would pick me up, anyway, and I'd rather starve out here than be behind bars. Used to be a mechanic in the Altoona railroad shops, but there isn't a thing doin' anywhere. A thousand men for every job. I get to places at six in the morning and they're already taken, and a big mob hangin' around outside. God! it's hell! I never knew I could get so low!

"How do I live? I don't know; parks, handouts, that sort of stuff. Haven't eaten for two days now, and was just getting to the point where I didn't care. God, look at all those autos going by, hundreds of them, all day. It makes me sick to look at 'em sometimes; people with money, and I don't know where I'm goin' to sleep to-night. I never knew the world could be like this!"

No one seems to know. He wrapped himself again in the obscurity of the doorway, and shivered in his lonely misery. Half a million men in the city, without friends, without women, without food and shelter, without a single one of the simple things that make Life bearable! And the city does not care. The preachers preach their sermons; the poets write their delicate lyrics; the business men sit in their fine offices, solemnly conducting the world's affairs; the politicians make fine speeches; the débutantes give their dances; the actors strut about the stages; the editorial writers ladle out words of wisdom; there is laughter, life, color, wine, wealth; the whole monstrous city moves down its primrose path, like a

The American Famine

courtesan plying her trade in the very shadow of the cross on which a Son of Man is writhing.

In Soviet Russia the famine can be endured. It is suffering that, not Society, but blind nature has imposed. Under the Red Flag, it will be solved. Under the Red Flag, it will not have been in vain; from their misery and death, a new bright world will grow like a garden well manured.

The Russian famine will end.

But there will be other famines in America; we are going nowhere; there is no plan; there is no vision.

DEATH OF A NEGRO

He was in the ward for only three days, but even at the end of the first day Miss Johnson had conceived a vast disgust for the Negro groaning in Bed Eight. The Negro was tall and powerful, over six feet of muscle and strength, with a handsome yellow manly face, and a voice deep and rich as a gong. He had been a longshoreman, and when carried in was still dressed in blue overalls; he was dirty and smelled of sweat and hard work. Even the longshoreman's pick was still in his belt, for he had been taken with acute appendicitis right at his job on the docks.

"Seems funny for a big husk lak me to get this, ain't it?" he mumbled cheerfully, as behind a screen Miss Johnson undressed him, sponged him, and got him into a fresh hospital nightgown. "Fust time Ah've evuh been sick in mah life, Lady, and dat's de Lawd's truth. Don't know what it's lak; but it cain't be so bad, now kin it?"

He was trying to be friendly, though in his pale face his teeth were chattering, and he was obviously suffering and frightened. Miss Johnson muttered some answer, and went on with her work.

"How often dey let visitors come for you here?" he continued, with his forced, cheerful smile. "Ah got a wife Ah'd give anything to see jes' now; seems lak a man is a big baby and wants his mammy or wife when he is took sick; now ain't dat so?"

"Yes," said Miss Johnson. "Now sit up for a moment; I want to put this nightgown over your head."

He lifted himself painfully, with her help, and his eyes, brown and pathetic, did not leave her face. He went on chatting, with affected gayety.

"This ain't so bad a sickness, this one of mine, is it? Ain't many dies of it, is they? They's good doctors here, too, ain't there? Dat's what the boys tole me; said the city pays foh you here, and treats you jes' right."

"You mustn't ask so many questions," Miss Johnson said.

"Oh, excuse me, excuse me!" the man said, flashing his brilliant white teeth. "Jes' a big baby, me; but you looked so nice an' kind, honey, Ah thought Ah could ask you something."

Miss Johnson's face was as cold as she could make it, and without another word she removed the screen, and went back to her little desk at the end of the room.

He had offended her. Miss Johnson was a big, kind American girl of about nineteen, immensely fat and overgrown, so that she seemed to burst through her uniform, and wore out shoes faster than the hospital supplied them. It was her second year of training; she had come from high school and home in a little Maine town, and though naïve and youthful, she had the rough charity and cheeriness of a strong country girl. No moods ever crossed her rosy, full-mooned face; in the midst of the daily horrors of the free ward the young girl was as calm and capable as an experienced mother. She even found innumerable occasions here for laughter, which she loved. Some favorite patient would make a witty remark, or have some mishap with the hospital paraphernalia, and great sounds of deep, healthy, contented laughter would roll from her; her sides would shake, the full, luscious flesh of her face would quiver; and two incongruously infantile dimples would form in her cheeks, making her resemble a swollen cherub. She was a happy girl. She did all the dirty work of a training nurse without a murmur of protest; death, filth and disease had become normal to her. There was a scrubby, baggy-eyed Greek barber in the ward with syphilis; and there was a tall Russian factory worker dying of necrosis of the jaw, and there were other sordid cases, but she treated them all with a smile. Physiology no longer offended her; but this familiarity of a Negro man did offend her, somehow. This was serious. He had called her "Honey."

After she went from his bedside, the smile left the Negro's face, and he looked about the ward with anxious eyes. He lay there studying it, as if it were a prison out of which he must ultimately have to break. There were ten beds on each side of the long, carpeted aisle, and in each of the dazzling white beds lay a pale man. Two patients at the end of his row were eating oranges and chatting soberly. A young Italian with a bandaged head was sitting up in bed and reading the comic pages of a Sunday newspaper. An old man with haggard, saffron face and silver hair had fallen asleep, and his gentle snoring filled the room. The nurse had gone back to reading her book; she sat at her desk. The sunlight fell in sheets through the many windows and lit the white walls and counterpanes with cheerful radiance. All was peaceful; but it did not soothe the Negro. He was suspicious and seemed to scent something; and he was in pain.

Suddenly he started, for the Russian with the rotting jaw had shrieked with delirium, and was trying to leap from his bed. The other patients stirred but slightly at the familiar sound. Miss Johnson rose leisurely, and pushed the great gaunt Russian back into bed. He cursed and spat like a foul, maddened cat, but she pressed him back calmly. The Russian's deep eyes were burning with madness; and he had a coarse, heavy, unshaven face, but Miss Johnson was not afraid of him. She soothed him. The Negro shuddered at those frightful howls, and felt the poisons in his own body leaping like fire. This was the house of death; he was trapped in it; he smelt the dull sickly odor of iodoform, and trembled at the faces of death around him. He was going to die. He wanted to scream like the Russian, but instead he called faintly:

"Kin I have a glass of water, ma'am?"

The plump young nurse rose wearily, with a little grunt, and brought him a glass of cold water. She set it on the table beside him, and started to return to her desk. Suddenly the Negro caught at her hand. She snatched it away, amazed at this impertinence.

"What's the matter?" she said sharply.

He was reaching again for her hand, naïvely, simply, with the confidence of a child.

"Ah ain't so bad, am I, ma'am? You see, Ah've nevah been sick befoh! Dis is all new to me, yessuh, jes' lak Ah jes' been born," and he tried to chuckle. Standing away from the bed, with a nervous frown on her fat, rosy, maternal face, Miss Johnson regarded him severely.

"You must keep your hands to yourself," she said. "If you want me to wait on you, you must remember that."

"Yas ma'am," he said. "When dey gwine op'rate on me?"

"To-morrow."

"You gwine be there when they op'rate on me?" he asked, still trying to chuckle.

"No, that's another nurse's work," she forced from reluctant lips.

"Dey gwine cut me up and take out my 'pendiseetus, hay?" he chuckled. "Seems lak dey want it; but dey kin have . . ."

Miss Johnson turned on her heel. She would not stand there and listen to these thinly disguised attempts at familiarity. The Negro looked after her like a frightened child. For half an hour he twisted and tossed, and then his body burned him so dreadfully, and he felt such fear, that he almost screamed again.

"Miss Nuss," he moaned, "won't you come here, please?"

She came to him. "What is it now?" she said.

"Mah feet are cold. Seems they're freezin'."

"You have enough blankets here." But she brought him a hot water bottle.

And twenty minutes had not passed when he was shaken by another spasm, and he called to her again, this time for a glass of water. As she gave it to him, he again made that amazing attempt to take her hand. Miss Johnson was almost frightened by such persistent familiarity.

He called on her almost every twenty minutes after that, and each time made the same feeble attempt to take her hand. She became so exasperated and nervous that she complained to the head nurse, when that erect, formal woman made her rounds.

"My gracious, Miss Adams, I can stand anything, I guess, but not that. I never knew Niggers were so crazy about white women, though I'd heard about it. He's been trying to get my hand all day; every time I've gone near him."

The head nurse went up to reprimand the Negro, but he was in another spasm, his eyes rolling wildly, his head twisting from side to side like a drunken man's. He was babbling incoherently: "Mammy! Mammy! Ah want my Mammy to come by me now, Mammy!"

"Just don't mind him," the head nurse said kindly. "We get such men occasionally; be dignified and aloof, and he will be impressed, and will not bother you."

The next morning the Negro was worse, and did not seem to notice Miss Johnson's attempts at dignity. He had been operated on at eleven o'clock, and after he came out of the ether, made more de-

mands than the day before, and as many attempts to
seize her hand. It got on her nerves; she spoke
sharply to him once or twice. The doctor had
ordered her to watch him closely, as a bad case of
peritonitis had been disclosed, and the Negro was
in bad shape. But her usual calm was ruffled; she
showed her irritation so much that the other patients
noticed the situation.

"That Nigger sure is in love with you," the young
Italian joked, winking a bright mischievous eye at
her. "Better look out, Miss Johnson, he sure after
you."

"It's he had better look out!" the fat nurse said
grimly, as she walked down the aisle with a bed-pan.
"I don't stand for such stuff from anybody!" The
old rheumatic dishwasher in the bed next the Italian's
lifted a friendly, roguish forefinger, and wagged it
at her. She did not smile, as she would have ordinarily. She felt humiliated that the other patients
were noticing the Negro's familiarities.

She talked it over with the night nurse, and with
some of her friends in the dormitory, and all of them
sympathized with her. The next morning she came
into the ward indignant and determined. She would
give the Negro the silent treatment nurses sometimes
use on patients they despise. She would ignore him
completely, except in the case of extreme necessity.
Let him ask for water all he wanted; he would get it
when she was ready. If he touched her hand again,
she would do nothing at all for him. The big black
bold alien, insolent and amorous, she would put him
in his place!

But something greater than Miss Johnson was putting the Negro into his place. It was Death. When Miss Johnson entered the ward, she saw in the sallow light of dawn a screen about the Negro's bed. The night nurse said he was dying. The poisons were eating his strong body like an acid; he was suffering a swift and terrible corruption of life. His groans sounded through all the ward that morning. The ward was still; there was not much talking or joking. Miss Johnson, in the midst of other duties, went behind the screen to watch the dying man. He seemed unconscious of her presence. In his weak, childish voice, once so deep and musical, like a gong, he called: "Mammy! Mammy!"

He was near the end. He was white as death, and she heard the rattle in his throat. He reached out for her hand, and now she let him have it. His touch was ice; she felt goose-flesh creeping over her from the contact.

"Oh Lawdie!" he murmured, and two big tears in his eyes shone as he died.

Miss Johnson did not change her opinion of him, however. That night she said to the nurse who came to relieve her: "That Nigger in Bed Eight died this morning. Funny about Niggers, isn't it, how they all want to make love to white girls? Gee, I can stand anything, I guess, but not that!"

FREE!

THE morning was spent in unwinding the yards of red tape that are woven into the steel chains of a prison. The four I.W.W. prisoners were checked through several offices, the warden spoke to them a moment or two, then they turned in their gray prison clothes and received in exchange their own forgotten creased clothes, stale after five years' repose in a bag. Then they were searched twice for contraband letters, then they were given their railroad tickets to Chicago, the city where they had been tried.

"So long, boys," one of the guards at the last steel door leading to the world, said jovially to them. He was a tall, portly, serene Irishman, with gray walrus mustaches, and he had seen hundreds of released men stand blinking like these four in the strange sunlight, dazed as if they had been fetched from the bottom of the sea. "So long, boys; drop in again some time when you're lonesome; we enjoyed your visit."

The men smiled awkwardly at him, stiffly and with the show of prison deference to a guard. They were still deferential and cautious like prisoners; in their minds they were not yet free.

They walked silently down the flat dusty road leading from the penitentiary to the highroad, their jaws set, their pale faces appearing unfamiliar and haggard to each other as their eyes glanced from side to side.

"So this is America!" said little Blackie Farrar,

heaving a deep sigh, and spitting hard and far into the road to display his nonchalance. Blackie was more nervous and trembly inside than any of the other men; but he could never forget that a man swaggers and grins and spits with a tough air when he is in a difficult situation. This blow of sudden freedom and sunlight after five years in prison fell harder upon Blackie than upon the other men. He had just come, the day before, from five months' solitary confinement in a black, damp underground cell, where he had been expiating the worst of prison offenses. He had battered with fists and feet a huge guard for the reason that this guard had been beating with fist, feet, black-jack and keys a weak, half-witted boy of nineteen who never seemed to remember his place in the line—another enormous prison crime.

"The land of the free and the home of the brave!" John Brown, a tall, lanky Englishman, with gray hair, hawk nose, and steady blue eyes added monotonously, as in a litany. "Wish I had a chew of tobacco!"

The other two I.W.W. prisoners, just released after their five years' punishment for the crime of having opposed a world war, did not say a word but stumbled along dumbly, as if waiting for something more interesting to happen. One was Hill Jones, a husky young western American, with the face and physique of a college football player, and with large luminous green eyes that stared at the world like those of an unspoiled child. The other I.W.W. was Ramon Gonzales, a young, slim, dark American-Mexican, the second generation of those hard-working Mexican peons who build the railroads of our western country.

"Wish I had a chew of tobacco!" repeated Brown, licking his dry lips with his tongue, and sweeping the brown drab prairie with his eyes. "Feel as if I could spit cotton!"

The truth was, he wanted the tobacco to steady his nerves. Like the others, he was quivering internally with a world of weird emotions. He had lived for five years in a steel house, behind steel bars, in a routine that was enforced by men with black-jacks and shotguns, and that was inhuman and perfect as steel. Now he was free. No one was watching him; he was strolling down a hot country road, under the immense yellow sky. He was back in the world of free men and free women; and he, and the others with him, should have breathed deeply, kissed the earth and rejoiced; instead they seemed tense and worried, a little disappointed.

What had they expected? They could not have said, but like all prisoners, they had built up, without knowing it, fantastic and exaggerated notions of the world outside. It seemed a little ordinary to them now. The sky was a dun yellowish waste with a sun shining through it. The wide dull prairie stretched on every hand like the floor of some empty barn, with shocks of gray rattling corn stacked in dreary rows, file after file to the horizon. A dog was barking somewhere. Smoke was rising from a score of farmhouses, and they heard the whistle of a distant freight train. There was dull burning silence on everything, the silence of the sun. The world of freedom seemed dull; but prisons are tense with sleepless emotions of hope and fear.

They were passing a farmer in a flannel shirt, plodding behind a team of huge horses in a field of stubble. His lean brown face was covered with sweat and fixed in grim, unsmiling lines as he held down the bucking plow and left a path of rich black soil behind him.

"Looks like a guy in for life, doesn't he?" said Brown, pointing to him with his thumb. "Looks like that murderer cellmate of yours, doesn't he, Ramon?"

The little Mexican cast a swift worried glance with his black eyes at the dull fanatic behind the plow.

"Yes," he said sharply, and stared back at the road beneath his feet.

"Same old goddamn corn," said Blackie, grinning, as he kicked a tin can out of the road, and spat, all in the same moment. "Same old goddamn Hoosiers, raising the goddamn corn! Corn and Hoosiers— God, why don't they raise a carrot once in a while?"

The others offered no answer to this American conundrum. They were moving on to fresh sights in this new world they had been thrust into—they were staring at the bend in the highroad where the town street began, two miles away from the prison. The ugly frame houses of the Middle West set among trees and smooth lawns, the trolley tracks, the stone pavements, then the stores and shop windows when they came nearer the heart of the town—that was what they saw. Up and down the streets men and women walked in the humdrum routine of life. A grocer was weighing out sugar in a dark window. They passed the little shop of an Italian cobbler. They passed a white school building, from which came the sound of fresh young voices singing. There was a line of Fords standing at the curb near the railroad depot. There were more women and men walking slowly about the square near the depot, discussing housework, and the election for sheriff and the price of corn and the price of hogs. This was the world.

"I don't see no brass bands out to meet us home," said Blackie, with his irrepressible grin. "How do you account for that, Hill? Ain't they heard we're coming?"

Hill, the young husky quarterback with the large green eyes, seemed unable to say a word. He scowled at Blackie, it seemed, and shook his head.

"What's the matter, Hill?" that worthy queried, with an insolent grin. "Ain't we as good as the boys who fought to make the world safe for democracy?"

"Aw, shut up!" Hill Jones muttered, "you get as talkative as a parrot sometimes!"

"I'm an agitator, that's why I talk," Blackie jeered, and would have said more, but that the Englishman Brown put his hand on Blackie's arm. There was a policeman loitering on the next corner, and for some strange reason, known only to ex-prisoners, the impassive Englishman was suddenly shaken to his soul.

"Let's get some coffee and," he said, leading them into the door of a cheap restaurant shaded by a wide brown maple tree. The four sat on stools against a broad counter loaded with plates of dessert, and looked into a mirror at their pale prison faces.

"Coffee and crullers," ordered the Englishman, naming the diet of all those who wander along the roads of America, and pick up their food like the sparrows where they can find it.

"Ham and eggs," said Hill.

"Ham and eggs and French fried and coffee," said Blackie.

"Ham and eggs," said Ramon, in a muffled voice.

The restaurant proprietor, a fat, cheerful man in a white apron had been counting dollar bills at his cash register and talking crops with a young farm hand in overalls. He locked the register with a sharp snap, and took their orders leisurely, the while guessing their status with his shrewd eyes. He repeated the orders into the little cubby hole leading to the kitchen.

"Solitary confinement, eh, what?" Blackie said to the Englishman, pointing at the forlorn, middle-aged face of the cook that peered out of the cubby hole, and repeated the orders in a voice from the tomb.

Neither Brown nor the others answered, but waited with grim patience for their food. When it came, they wolfed it down rapidly, as if some one were watching them. Blackie could not be still, however.

"This is better than the damn beans and rotten stew every day at the other hotel," he muttered. "Real ham and eggs! Oh, boy!"

Brown looked at the clock. It was just noon. "I

guess the boys are having their grub now," he said.
"Yes, there goes the whistle. Gosh, you can hear it all the way over here!"

Yes, it was the prison whistle, the high whining blast like the cry of some cruel hungry beast of prey, rising and falling over the little town and all the flat corn-lands, the voice of the master of Life, the voice of the god of the corn-lands. The four prisoners in this restaurant knew that call well; and every one in the town and every one living on the corn-lands knew it as thoroughly as they did.

"Look," said Blackie, pointing through a window behind them, "you can just see the top of the prison walls from here. Who would have thunk you could see it so far?"

The men turned from their food to stare gloomily, while the fat proprietor hid a knowing smile behind his curled mustaches.

"Two thousand guys in hell," said Jones quietly, "and all these Hoosiers think about is corn and hogs. Twenty-five of our boys still in there, ninety-six still in Leavenworth—God, why do we let ourselves be crucified by these Hoosiers?"

"Jim Downey's got fifteen more years to go; so has Frank Varrochek, Harry Bly, Ralph Snellins and four others," said John Brown quietly, piercing with his deep blue eyes through all the distance. "And Jack Small has consumption; and George Mulvane is going crazy—Hill, do you think we'll ever get 'em out alive?"

Ramon suddenly became hysterical.

He stood up with brandished fists and shook them

at the distant prison, quivering with the rage of five years of silence. His olive face darkened with blood, and locks of his long raven-black hair fell in his eyes, so that he could not see. He flamed into sudden Latin eloquence.

"Beasts!" he cried, in a choked furious voice, "robbers of the poor, murderers of the young; hangmen, capitalists, patriots; you think you have punished us! You think we will be silent now, and not speak of your crimes! You can never silence us! You can torture us, you can keep us in prison for all of our lives—"

"Oh, Ramon," Blackie cried, pushing him back into his seat, and patting him soothingly on the shoulder. "Easy, easy! We all feel as sore as you do, Ramon, and we hate them just as hard. By God, we hate them. But easy now, old-timer, easy!"

The others helped quiet the nerve-racked young Mexican, and he finally subsided and sat there with his face between his hands until they had finished their food. Then the four paid their check to the amused but discreet fat proprietor, and went into the street on their way to the railroad station, trying again to appear casual and unconcerned.

At the next corner another policeman was lounging against a store window, and it was with an effort that each of the freed men passed his vacant eye. They braced up and walked by bravely, but they still found it hard to believe that they were really free.

It would take them some months to become accustomed to the greater prison house known as the world.

BOUND TO GET HOME

MAKINS BUTLER was a short, brawny Negro in a hickory shirt and blue overalls, a migratory worker with a pleasant face and misty, dog-like eyes. He had ranged all over the western lands during his five years on the road. There are thousands like him in the West, wandering from harvest to harvest, living like homeless dogs. But Makins was homesick for the South; he was tired of being a hobo.

"No, suh," he said in the bunk-house at the Californian fruit ranch one night, "hain't nuthin' lak South Carolina in all the world. Got my folkses there, and a little yaller gal or two Ah kin have any time Ah says the word. It's a good livin' down there, Ah'll tell ye, boy! Don't make as much jack as here, mebbe, but hain't the beatin's a hobo gets along the road. Ah don't lak this hoboin' around business, nohow; hit's a yaller-pup life, it is. Ah've been beaten up fohty-six times, Ah'll bet, time sence Ah've been on the road."

His friend, a powerful, easy-going black giant, roared with laughter and hit Makins a huge slap on the shoulder. They called him Makins because he was always borrowing Bull Durham "makings" for cigarettes from the other men.

"Well, why don't ye just a-travel South?" the friend laughed. "Who's a-holdin' ye, Makins?"

Makins grinned shamefacedly. "No one a-holdin'

Bound To Get Home

me," he admitted. "Jes' a damn fool, me, wid not the sense of a horse-fly in mah fool haid! Every time Ah gets a stake to go back with Ah jest fritters it away. Ah've started fohty-nine times for South Caroline, Ah guess, and never gone through. Always frittered mah stake away fust, lak a bo'n baby."

But one day, with a hundred dollars stuck safely in his shoes, Makins made another start for South Carolina. He made a fast freight, and spread himself royally in a boxcar on some straw. He smiled and chatted with himself as he felt the long miles clicking off beneath him; saw through the half-open door the deserts and ranches and mountains of the West marching by. He was happy. He was going home with a stake at last. His mammy, if she were still alive, would be proud of him; he would live like a lord for the next six months.

"Gawd, why hain't Ah done this befoh?" he chuckled to himself. "Nevah had no sense, me; always a bo'n fool. One time Ah spends mah stake on whisky; 'nuther time lets a slick nigger trim me with loaded dice; 'nuther time, that Filipino gal, she jest cleans me out; jes' a bo'n fool, me! But hain't no one nor nuthin' goin' stop me this time, no, suh! Hain't a-goin' to be stopped this trip!"

He would have broken into joyful Negro thanksgiving and song had he not remembered that the trip was not yet over. He was still on the road, in the enemies' country. Hoboes lead a rough and dangerous life. Hoboes are beaten up frequently; when they are Negroes as well as hoboes they are hounded, arrested, tortured, robbed and beaten up twice as frequently. Makins traveled anxiously for three days, but nothing happened to him.

"Nothin' goin' to stop me this trip!" he chuckled to himself over and over again like an incantation.

One afternoon, in the Arizona desert, Makins forgot to smile and chat to himself as he sprawled in the boxcar straw. The train was nearing a little junction town named Maricopa. This was the home of Maricopa Slim, a railroad detective famous with all the western hoboes for his love of whisky and his mania for "sapping up" hoboes, sap being the western name for blackjack. Many a hobo had felt Slim's sap on his head and ribs; the town was avoided by the wise boxcar traveler.

Makins had heard all about Slim. He prepared for the famous butcher of defenseless hoboes. He shut the door of the car, and huddled miserably in a dark corner. They were nearing Maricopa now. The long freight train stopped with a rattle and a bang; voices were mumbling outside; yes, this was the junction. Beads of clammy sweat came out on Makins' forehead.

"Nuthin's goin' to happen to me on this trip!" he said over and over again for consolation.

But something did happen. The door was slid back abruptly on its rollers, and a tall, brick-faced westerner in sombrero and riding pants loomed there. He flashed his pocket lamp about the dusky car. He found Makins crouching in a corner, and smiling, dragged him forth into the sunlight of the railroad yard. Makins shrunk into a ball, tumbled out without a word.

It was Maricopa Slim, all right. Standing over the Negro, he smiled again. His raw, beefy face was flushed with drink. He looked pleased. But then he kicked Makins in the thigh with his heavy boot. "Get the hell out of this town, ye Nigger bastard!" he suddenly snarled, like a stage villain. "Comin' in here to make work for me!"

He took a tight merciless grip on Makins' shirt and walked him in silence for about a mile through the town. They came to the colony of Mexican shacks where the town met the desert. Makins dragged along, depressed and yet a little hopeful. The tall red-faced detective was just going to put him out of the town limits, that was all. A few hours lost, but no beating, he thought.

"Now get the hell out of this town, ye Nigger bastard!" the detective repeated, letting go his hold on Makins' collar, and kicking him forward. Makins did not answer a word, but started to walk quickly toward the wide blazing horizon. Got off easy at that, he thought. Suddenly he was felled by a cruel blow from behind him. Maricopa Slim had begun on his favorite sport. He slugged the prostrate Negro with his blackjack over the head and face; the blood that spurted excited him, and he slugged the Negro again. Then he kicked Makins in the face, and stamped on him with both feet, and finally spat at him, then walked away, mopping his forehead.

Makins lay on the desert sand, unconscious for an

hour. The sun beat on him; the flies gnawed at his raw flesh. When he came to, he moaned and felt himself. He found gashes and bruises everywhere. He sat up and slowly began thinking about it all. Fury seized him; it seemed to him as if the past five years had been nothing but this sort of life. A terrible rage swept over him; his eyeballs grew red and inflamed, he stood up and shook his fists toward the town.

"Always sappin' ye up, always beatin' ye up!" he cried hysterically. "Ah'll kill this bastard; Ah'll go down to Bowie and buy me a gun and come back and kill that bastard! No one hain't a-goin' to sap me up again! Dis is de last time!"

Towards dusk he caught a train at a water tank, and it was going to Bowie. He lay in the straw, weak and bleeding, and filled with a tearful, murderous frenzy. "Ah'll buy me a gun in Bowie, and jest go back and kill him, that's what Ah'll do! Always sappin' ye up, always beatin' ye up!"

He reached Bowie in the night, and got a room in a cheap hotel where he washed his face and hands and had something to eat. Then he went out into the streets, brooding, "Ah'll get a gun now! Ah'll get me a gun!" But as he walked about, little by little his rage departed. There were so many redfaced westerners in sombreros who looked like Maricopa Slim, and as he passed them, he felt each of them as ready to sap him up as Slim had been. The dimly lit streets were crowded with these devils; the world was full of them.

"Oh, hain't no use," he found himself saying

wearily at last. "No use monkeyin' around, Makins; don't spend no money on no gun, or waste yoh time. Jest get back South to you people, that's what you want. Nuthin's goin' to stop you on this trip, no suh, nuthin'; jest bound to get home!"

TWO MEXICOS

THE world was beautiful as we rode out from Guadalajara in the golden morning light. The broad Mexican spaces were blazing with color, with the glistening green of new corn and the dull green of cactus, with the fire of yellow sands and the slow, blue radiance of meadows thronged with trees. Nothing seemed solid; all was radiance; the world was the heart of a crystal ball of radiance.

Far off on the horizon loomed the mountains—the grand, savage, naked hills of Mexico, that stand everywhere like the visible passion of the land—great, glorious masses of rock cut in fantastic patterns, all barren of vegetation like jewels, and shining like them in purple, amber and rose.

The air sparkled. From the blue perfect sky, winds came against our faces, intoxicating as flowers. The horses sniffed the freshness of the morning, and stepped springily over the gaps in the road, and down the rocky inclines on our way to Don Felipe's ranch, thirty miles from the city.

Don Felipe was gay, and we, too, were gayer than careless birds as we jogged through that thrilling Mexican countryside, that is always like some melodrama of color and form planned by a wild young master. We drank the winds greedily, and filled our eyes with the pageant about us, and felt strongly the mad joy of living. Don Felipe burst into song,

Two Mexicos

and, clapping spurs to his horse, went roaring down the road for a few hundred yards. Then he wheeled violently and came charging back at us in a spectacular cloud of dust.

"*Viva Mejico!*" he shouted, swinging his fringed sombrero about his head, and whooping like an Indian. "Have you anything so wonderful as this in the United States?"

"No, no!" we cried, carried away by the high, reckless, romantic mood that the Mexican landscape induces in the beholder.

Felipe reined his horse in beside ours, and, digging into his saddle-bag, brought out a bottle of the white, incandescent liquor named *tequila*. We accepted a pull at the stuff, and Felipe gurgled a great mouthful of the flaming mixture himself, his tanned face red as a poppy when the *tequila* entered his veins.

Felipe was a friend of three days' acquaintance. Joe and I had fallen in with him while lounging about the *Fama Italiana*, the only good café in the sunlit, sweet-smelling, church-ridden city of Guadalajara. Felipe could speak a choppy and slangy English he had picked up in one of the American border towns. His ancestry was undoubtedly Spanish, for he had blue, bulging eyes, a tawny mustache and crop of hair, and a big, curved, Oriental nose, tenderly pink at the tip, and unlike the sharp, razor noses that mark the Aztec strain. He was short, natty and slender, and unbelievably wiry, like a young tiger. He had come into town on business, and had spent almost a week on the spree that accompanied every transaction of his. Now, when he was returning to the ranch, he had insisted that we go with him for a visit. We, ready for anything, went.

"You will like our ranch!" he said, as he trotted his horse beside us, sitting lightly in the high, elaborate saddle, a dazzling figure in the *charro* costume he changed to from the neat Chicago business suit he had worn in the city.

"It's not a large ranch, as Mexican estates go, but we have everything for your entertainment—wild deer to shoot, a mountain pool always cold as ice, horses to ride, and many nearby places you will enjoy seeing. You will like it, I know. We employ about a hundred *peones* on the ranch, and raise corn, wheat, maguey and cattle. You will see how we lasso steers and brand them. We will give a fiesta in your honor, you will have many pretty girls to dance with. What more do you want? You have but to say it, and it is yours!"

He waved his hand in a large, free flourish, and we thanked him for his hospitality.

"I and my brother Enrique own the ranch," he continued. "Our father left it to us; I am the elder brother. You will like my brother Enrique. He is a strong, fearless, honest man—much better than I am, but too serious. He takes life as if it were a religion, but to me, *Caramba!* it is one great joke! I laugh at it! That is the right way, no?"

He fished out the *tequila* bottle and slapped it fondly, then offered us another draught of the liquor.

"No, thank you!" both of us said. "The American stomach isn't strong enough for Mexican *tequila* and a Mexican horse at the same time."

Felipe laughed uproariously. "Ha, ha, ha!" he shouted, hitting his thigh, "that is true, that is true! I have seen many Gringoes put under the table by our *tequila!* That is one point where we Mexicans will always have the better of you!" He swallowed another long drink, and wiping his lips, put the bottle away.

"Would you believe it," he said earnestly, leaning forward to us from his saddle, "my brother Enrique will not touch a drop of alcohol—not a drop. He is a fanatic on the subject. He goes so far that he has wished to give up our *maguey* fields, from which the *pulque* is made that the poor people drink. But I would not let him do this, and he can do nothing without my consent. If I let him have his way, we would be ruined in a year, he has such fantastical ideas on everything. Just the same, he is a good man, a real man—and the best rider and lassoer on the ranch; better even than I!"

A shade of somber intensity crossed his face, to be immediately followed by the mood of bold, reckless laughter—violent mirth playing scornfully with life and death, and heedless of a single human value. That was how we found Felipe—there were depths in him, some chords that could be touched, but dominant was the full tide of his barbarianism, his strange lack of the sense of good and evil, his paganism stained with the blood of a creed that makes manslaughter a trifle light as love.

Felipe lived but to drink, to win women, to ride

horses and to prove his personal valor in contest with other strong barbarians. He was proud and sensitive; and as unconsciously cruel as an animal. He told stories of his exploits on the ride through that glowing, great scene, and we listened to him in fascinated amazement, as to some dark man from the Middle Ages.

"Once," he said, "we had a young peasant on our ranch who had conceived a fierce hatred for me. He was a steady, hard-working fellow, living with his parents, and in love with one of the peon girls for whom I had taken a fancy, and whom I managed to seduce. The fellow heard of this, and it made him begin to hate me.

"You must understand that before the Revolution the workers on the ranch were really our slaves. They owned nothing of their own, and they had to take what we gave them. They could not leave the estates of their masters, for they were always in debt to us. We did anything we pleased with them —there was no law. When they approached us on business they would kiss our hands.

"Now it is different. Now the peons live on our property, rent free, and work for wages. We pay them about 25 cents daily, and on this they manage to save a little and buy fancy revolvers and sewing machines and other luxuries that turn their heads. It is the result of this accursed Revolution that has upset everything.

"My brother, I must tell you, has even tried to go out of his way to turn the heads of the peasants. He gives them a bonus out of the profits at the end of the year, and he gives them little fields where they can cultivate their own produce. He is quite insane on this subject. He has read books. He treats the peons almost like equals. Once he wanted to turn our entire ranch over to them, with himself as mere manager and servant to them. I came to blows with him almost before I could drive this mad notion out of his head. He fought in the Revolution, you see— he was one of the first to risk his life for it, and one of the few who really believed in it, and who did not try to grab a fat political job for his services. He is a good man, my brother, but a little mad. He worships a book written by a mad Russian named Tolstoy.

"Well, to come back to my story, this peon, a tall, dark, silent fellow, began showing his hatred for me soon after he learned I had had his girl. He would scowl at me when I passed, and refused to take off his hat to salute me, as every peon on our ranch must, when I go by. Once I sprang off my horse and tore his hat from his head, and flung it on the ground.

" 'You must never fail to salute your betters!' I cried, sticking my revolver under his nose. 'Do you understand that?'

" 'Yes!' he said quietly, turning on his heel and leaving the hat there in the road.

"His bravado and insolence maddened me, and I wanted to shoot him in the back as he walked away. Perhaps I would have done so, but the thought came to me it would be better to let the beast live and to make his life a misery for him. Thus I would show him who the better man was, and at the same time it would give a practical lesson to the other peons, who were quite as bad as he was. It is the only method, my friends; you must daily show these cattle of the fields that you are their master; you must do it frankly and harshly; they do not understand other methods. Ah, if my brother were not only my brother, I could show the way to keep these dogs down!

"Well, to make a long story short, this Pedro meekly bore all the insults and hardships I put upon him. I once lashed him with my whip across the face, while he was working in the fields with the other peasants. I came to his cottage one day and took five of his chickens and wrung their necks before him, and walked away. We needed meat for dinner that day, you see; I did other things to humiliate him, but he said nothing. Perhaps he found it inconvenient to move with his parents from the ranch, I do not know. It may be he was making up with the girl again, and thought of marrying her before he left.

"Anyway, I came across the two one Sunday, talking in front of the church at Tonala, where we go for mass. There was a group of the peons from our ranch there, lounging about under the trees and waiting for the services to begin. I dashed up to the two lovers, and seizing the girl around the waist, swung her on my horse and rode off with her. Pedro stood looking after me with the most stupid eyes you ever saw.

"The next day he did not come to work. I was passing his cottage in the morning on my way to the wheat fields, when he sprang out from behind a stone wall and fired a revolver at me. His face was white with anger, and he did not speak a word. The shot grazed my shoulder, and I leaped on him, and dug my knife into his ribs and killed him. Then I found a rope and hung him to a tree, where every one could see him as an example. All on the ranch, when they saw him later, knew I had killed him, but no one dared to lay the case before the officials at Tonala, for these are my friends. Ah, but my brother was angry with me then! We almost fought with guns that time!"

He laughed reminiscently, and spurred his horse into a proud, slow trot, with the foam coming from the checked animal's mouth. We were rather shocked by the story, but knew no way of breaking in on the man's unconsciousness of the evil of his deed. Besides, there was a curious atmosphere about him as he told these things that eliminated all feeling of morality; he was like some returned soldier who narrates dreadful horrors and murders to an audience that shudders and yet cannot blame. Life seems different and younger on these passionate Mexican plains; death is as casual and unimportant here as it is to a child. We hardly knew what to say, and rode on in thoughtful silence.

In Felipe, on his glossy, splendid horse, in his flamboyant leather costume with its silver buttons and rich decorative cordings, we seemed to see riding the incarnation of that brutal, primitive aristocracy that had weighed the Mexican worker to the dust, and that we had found still dominant wherever we had been in the Republic. It was the incarnation of all the thoughtless evil of the Latin and Indian nature, sanguinary, haughty, passionate, and lust-loving, with no mercy for the animal or man in its power. It was too proud to be hypocritical about its vices or virtues; it was the pure primitive.

We grew anxious to meet Felipe's brother Enrique. For only one sober thread of conscience had we detected in the scarlet pattern of Felipe's nature, and that was his feeling for his brother. Always in the stories Felipe dropped from time to time the brother appeared as some better angel, sad, striving and impotent before Felipe's savageries. Felipe would always say his brother was mad, but we could find in him, too, a faint spark of shame and unworthiness that made him uneasy when he spoke of the other. It was as if he knew his brother was right, but could not acknowledge it or live up to his brother's ideals, and for this reason assumed a cloak of exaggerated boyish superiority that ill-fitted him. His brother was Felipe's external conscience, his sole link to the goodness that is in Mexico.

The sun was climbing high into the sweep of glittering sky. Heat waves shimmered like the hot breath of the sandy, scrubby wastes about us. A few grouse could be heard whirring in the shade of a yucca-tree off the road. Felipe unslung his rifle and drew a bead on the speckled creatures. He did not shoot, however, for a thought crossed his mind.

"Ah! I forgot; we must not waste time!" he said, dropping his gun. "We are expected at the ranch, I think. Let us keep moving."

Two Mexicos 103

This was a good resolution, and Joe and I felt cheered by it. We had started from town soon after dawn, and were due at the ranch about two in the afternoon, but Felipe had developed vagaries that ate up the hours. We were saddle-weary and hungry.

He set his horse off into a good trot and we followed, but our hopes of reaching the ranch sank only a few minutes later, never again to rise. Felipe stopped, and took another drink from the bottle. His eyes lit with enthusiasm. The serious purpose on his face was wiped off, as with a sponge. He pointed to a dark-green meadow criss-crossed by irrigation ditches, a few levels below us in the valley.

"See the bulls there!" he cried gleefully. "Now I will show you how Mexicans can ride! We have lots of time!"

He spurred his horse over a fence, and into the meadow where a herd of cattle was peacefully grazing. With wild cries he lassoed a huge black bull by the hind legs, and, leaping off his horse, fastened a rope around the animal's middle. The bull was furious, but Felipe leaped on its back, and holding tight to the rope, gripped his legs into the creature's side, and lashed it into a frothing rage with his sombrero.

The bull put its head down and charged like an express train. It shook itself from side to side, and bucked and came down on all its four hoofs. It bellowed madly, but Felipe held on as if glued, and shouted and even had the bravado to take both hands from the precious rope to wave his hat at us. The bull tried to scrape him off against the stone fence of the corral—it tried every trick its slow brain could devise. Then it came at last to a weary and bewildered halt, breathing hard. Felipe leaped lithely from its back. He recovered his rope and returned to us. He was grinning, and ill-concealed vanity shone in his fishy blue eyes.

"What do you think of that?" he asked in a glow, taking another pull at the unfailing bottle. We assured him we had never seen anything like it before.

The trip was resumed, down a gentle valley, then up a circular path that ascended a hill all of grass, on whose round summit a little square block-house stood, a memento of the Revolution. Felipe showed us some of the trenches the fighters had made, and pointed out some mounds marked by faded wooden crosses, the graves of the revolutionists.

"That is their reward, the fools!" he said, "and that is all they deserved to get! I often tell my brother that."

He seemed in no hurry to get home now, though the morning was advancing toward noon and the sun was stronger on our backs. It was amazing what animal spirits the man had—life overflowing and exuberant and positively aching for expression. He roared lovely sad Spanish songs, he beat his horse into wild gallops and trots, he drank from the bottle and told us story after story of violence and lust. He was tireless, athirst for danger, like a bored mountain lion.

We scrambled down a *barranca*, a deep mountain

gorge whose paths were steep alleys of bowlders on which the horses slipped and floundered. Sheer thousand-foot drops were on one hand of us, and on the other were rugged cliffs black and wet with hidden springs. Felipe would not permit his horse to pick its careful, difficult way through the stones, but whipped it on blindly, and bade us follow. Once he jumped his horse over a chasm that we went painfully around, his poor beast sliding and crashing, and almost toppling over the cliff. Felipe laughed, and looked at us for admiration.

At the bed of the *barranca* rushed a full, strong mountain-river, deep and foaming yellow. Felipe insisted that we all strip for a swim, and we saw him dive recklessly into the rocky bottom, and fight his way out of that great, steep cup of savage bowlders and stunted shrubbery. We climbed the other side of the mountain. At the top we found a green, immense valley stretched beneath us, a tremendous plain of shining grass and dark clots of trees, threaded by silver rivers. The huge, billowy shadows of clouds moved over its brilliant face. The plain was beautiful in its broad peace, a wonderful stage set for Titans, and far off in a corner we saw a cluster of white houses from which a church-tower rose, like the pistil of a flower. Felipe had stopped his horse, and was gazing thoughtfully.

"That must be the ranch there!" we cried, pointing to the distant houses. Felipe shook his head.

"No," he said thoughtfully, "that is the village of Tonala, about four miles from the ranch. Do you know what would be a good idea?" he added slowly, his face lighting with enthusiasm. "We ought to go there and not to the ranch for our dinner. We are hungry, and besides, I have some important business to transact there."

"Are you sure of that, Felipe?" we asked, trying to divert him from we knew not what.

"Carajo!" he exclaimed, "of course I am sure! The Judge at Tonala has sent our ranch a requisition for five saddled horses, to be used for two months by the military commander who is fighting the rebels. I know what they will do with those horses; they will sell them. I must go and have the order withdrawn."

"But how can you do that?" Joe asked.

"How?" Felipe laughed, tugging at his reddish mustache. "How? *Bueno,* I will get the Judge drunk! Wait and see!"

So we urged the horses onward to the pueblo of Tonala. The valley grew richer and greener as we went cantering down the rough roads, there were more trees, and cultivated fields, and squat adobe houses with their little gardens and cactus fences enclosing a few pigs or a cow or two. At last the road became a street lined with these little houses side by side, the plaster walls painted in delicate shades of pink and blue. We were in Tonala; a village of about 500 peon inhabitants, the center of all the farms in the valley. Lounging men in white peon clothes and immense hats stared somberly as we clattered by, children scattered about us, peon women looked up from ditches where they squatted at their laundering.

Felipe preened himself with his usual vanity,

Two Mexicos

combed his hair and mustache. We whipped up the horses, and entered at a spectacular gallop into the grass-grown, sleepy plaza that is the heart of every Mexican town.

We had a dinner of beefsteak, eggs, frijoles and black coffee at a small restaurant, bare as a cell, and presided over by an unimaginably old and wrinkled crone. Then Felipe led us to his business with the Judge.

We found this dignitary sitting in the sunshine on a bench in front of his home, doggedly playing Mexican waltzes on a mandolin, to which the Sheriff played accompaniments on a guitar. The Judge was a battered little old man, with matted gray hair and beard, and tiny stupid eyes that twinkled suspiciously, like a weasel's. He was clad in the white, cotton flapping clothes of an ordinary peon, his dirt-caked feet enclosed in sandals. From out of the wild tangle of hair on his face a corn-husk cigarette drooped, stale and forgotten.

The Sheriff was huge and burly, with an enormous black mustache that almost reached to his eyes. He too was dressed in peon clothes, with a red blanket folded over his right shoulder, and a shirt of vivid flowered pink made by his wife of gaudy calico. Around the Sheriff's waist was a heavy belt loaded with cartridges, and a 30-30 rifle stood against the wall by his side. The officials abandoned their harmonizing as we came up, and arose to greet us.

"Felipe, my friend!" the Judge called in a cracked, joyful voice, embracing our host in the Mexican style and patting his shoulder enthusiastically. "Why have I not seen you for so long?"

The proper introductions were made, there was some small talk, then Felipe drew the Judge aside and held a serious conversation with him. We could tell this by the solemn air with which the two conversed, and the manner in which the Judge shook his head from side to side, as if in doubt. Finally Felipe took him by the arm and brought him over to us.

"Let us all go to the *cantina!*" Felipe said. "We need something to drink."

The Sheriff bowed gravely and picked up his rifle and walked. We followed, leading our horses, and crossed the little plaza to a low, ill-smelling wooden shack painted with great letters in red and blue, reading, "La Lucha Por La Vida"—The Struggle for Life. That is the romantic way Mexican merchants name their dingy little dry-goods and grocery establishments.

Inside the *cantina* there was a wooden counter, sticky with liquor and swarming with flies. Behind this were shelves with various colorful bottles standing in rows, and a huge barrel containing the oily, sour, thin drink called *pulque*. A few peons drooped about cheerfully, and the saturnine, fat man behind the counter greeted us with the universal bartender's smile. Felipe ordered drinks for every one, striking the bar with his fist.

"This is our holiday," he cried, "and no one must be unhappy!"

We drank the *tequila*. Tongues began loosening after the third or fourth drink, laughter arose as if by magic. Confidences began.

The Sheriff spoke to us solemnly, from the heart. "You have many wonderful things in the United States, you Gringoes," he said to us, "but there is one thing of ours you cannot have, and that is our National Hymn. It is the most beautiful hymn in the world. Did you know," he informed us proudly, "did you know that once the United States offered ten million dollars if we would give them our hymn for their own, but that we refused? Yes, we refused, for we are poor, but men of honor and sentiment and pride. And this is a fact, it is history; my own brother heard from a policeman he knew well in Guadalajara."

They sang the national hymn, which is really beautiful, beating on the counter with their glasses. There were other songs, and stories of women and fighting. The Judge was not holding his liquor well, for his little eyes were growing dimmer and dimmer, and he wobbled on his feet.

"The Revolution set us peons free," he uttered in a hazy voice, slapping his chest. "Yes, we are free now. Do you see, I am the Judge here, and if any one should hurt person or property in this pueblo I would instantly put him in jail. No robbers, no atheists, no reactionaries are allowed here. If we find a rebel, we hang him at once. We are free!"

"You, Señor, are the best Judge in the whole state of Jalisco, aren't you?" Felipe said, putting his arm on the little man's shoulder and winking at us.

"Yes!" the Judge answered at once, glaring at him half-suspiciously. "Yes, I am! And here is the best Sheriff in the whole state of Jalisco!"

The Sheriff swelled out his chest, and lifted his gun to his lips and kissed it religiously.

"With this gun I maintain the law and order in this village!" he proclaimed, beginning to wobble a little too. "I have arrested three drunks to-day and not one dared to put up a fight. They know who I am."

Drink after drink, and the shadows gathered in the room and obscured the wild, flushed Indian faces. Outside the door the blue sky caught the last flame from the sun, and then dusk came down. The trees were liquid darkness, and deep soft rich darkness filled the dusty street. Our horses champed impatiently. We went outside, calling Felipe after us.

"Aren't you ready to go yet?" we asked politely. "Haven't you arranged that matter of the horses with the Judge?"

"Yes, I've arranged it all!" he said excitedly. "We'll have a few more drinks and go. Come in!"

We returned reluctantly, and continued drinking, for it is almost an insult to refuse an offer of this kind in Mexico.

The place grew wilder and noisier as the liquor mounted to all heads. Felipe began boasting, and drew his large hunting-knife from its scabbard, and stuck it into the counter.

"This is my only friend!" he cried, "with its aid I can do what I choose anywhere. I have killed three men with it, and am ready for more—at any time, even now!"

"But you will keep order in *this* village, Señor!"

the Judge mumbled stupidly, moving up against Felipe and fronting him chest to chest.

"I will do what I choose!" Felipe sneered, waving the knife in the air. "I have a ranch of three leagues, and employ a hundred peons. I will do what I please!"

"No!" the Judge shouted, flushing with anger. "No! Arrest that man!"

But it was the Judge that the Sheriff took by the arm and forcibly led out into the night. "I will keep law and order here!" the Sheriff mumbled grandly, dragging the smaller man as if he were a sack of flour. "I am the Sheriff here, you must remember!"

The two came back a moment later, and Felipe bought them many more drinks. Joe and I went outside, weary, our heads whirling. We waited for Felipe there. At last he staggered to us, after many hours of night, when the village was all darkness and dots of lamplight, and the stars had long crowded the sky. He mounted his horse, and we started off.

The Judge and Sheriff stood waving their hands after us. As we rode down the rocky street we could see their dark, wavering forms in the moonshine. We reached a great tree where the street changed to fields. Felipe turned on his horse and fired three shots toward the *cantina*. A great crash answered, a bullet sped by us somewhere, and we saw a fiery burst of flame spring where the Sheriff was standing in darkness. The friends were saluting each other.

We rode through rich moonlight, between fields of corn that glistened like waves of the night-sea. The distant mountains stood blue and smoky against the sky. The air was more exciting than love. A world of mystery lay about us; the drink was in our blood, and the wind against our faces. We shouted and sang. Felipe shot his revolver off many times, and we followed with salutes to the dreaming sky. It was romance to be alive, it was ecstasy and adventure, and the sad Mexican earth, humble beneath us in the moonlight, rang again and again with cries of our reckless joy.

Felipe was in glorious mood. We too had forgotten everything in abandonment of reckless wonder. Felipe saw something stirring in the bush, and shot his revolver at it. The next moment an old, bent peon came out, and stood bowing in fright. We laughed madly, and sped on our way.

We spurred our horses over great bowlders, and across a stream, and through soft purple meadows sweet to the nostrils. The moonlight drowned all the senses in silver. There were millions of colored stars in the Mexican sky. Little adobe houses swam by us in the night, boats on a dark magic river. The mountains were before us. It was the greatest moment of my life.

Then, jumping a fence, and walking our horses through the corduroy roughness of a plowed field, we came upon the houses of the ranch quietly glowing under the moon. Felipe fired another shot, and cried, "We're home!"

We set our horses into a furious gallop, and with flushed faces and beating hearts roared up to the biggest house of all, where the brothers lived. Felipe banged out another shot, still shouting, *"Viva Mejico!"*

A tall, solemn figure came out on the porch as we reined in our horses. It was Felipe's brother Enrique. He had dark, stern Indian features, and a stiff, black mustache. He folded his arms and regarded us out of lowered eyes. His silence was ominous, and chilled our joy with a cold hand.

Felipe seemed to sober up and became somewhat sheepish under that gaze. We dismounted, and went up on the porch where Enrique stood. He fixed Felipe with his black, grave, dangerous eyes.

"You drunkard!" Enrique said, in a low, fierce voice. "You drunkard! You care for nothing but your pleasures and passions! You have been away three days now! You have probably spent all the money for the corn you sold!"

Felipe's face flamed with badly suppressed rage. "I am the elder brother here," he muttered; "you can say nothing to me!"

"You drunkard!" the other repeated bitterly. "All that I do here you undo. You and your kind are the curse of our poor Mexico! Follies such as yours have been the ruin of our people. If you weren't my brother I would kill you!"

"I am the elder brother here!" Felipe muttered sullenly, his hand twitching at his revolver.

They stood facing each other in the vast, silent

moonlight, the brothers who were the poetry and wisdom of Mexico, her good and evil, her barbarism and civilization battling each other and assuring her no peace till the younger shall have forever slain the elder.

ON A SECTION GANG

The paycar eased alongside. We threw down our tools and fell in line by the track. Through the steel-barred window the cashier handed the sunburnt section gang its pay envelopes.

Every one was happy; every one grinning; even Rich, our hard-boiled foreman, cracked a smile. Every one relaxed; there was a lot of horseplay.

Sure, it was a great victory for the section gang. The company was presenting them with two weeks' pay. They acted as foolish and grateful, those giant children, as if it were a gift.

Pay day—pay—it's the opium of the masses.

And the gang spent most of it by the next morning.

We covered an eighth of a mile a day on Section 10. We tore out rotten old ties as we went along, and put in new ones.

First you shoveled out the old cinder ballast. Then you pried your crowbar under the old spikes, and leaned on the long hunk of steel with all your bone and gristle, until the rusty five-inch spike came out groaning like a big tooth.

Then you dragged out the old tie and rolled it over the bank. Then you jockeyed the new tie, dripping with creosote, into the old bed. Then you swung a ten-pound sledge, Wham! Wham! on the head of the new spike, until it seemed to grow into the wooden tie. Then you shoveled back the cinder ballast, and tamped it down.

For about a month half the gang was covered with boils. I was miserable with twelve. We figured at first it was the drinking water, but Rich the Foreman told us it was the creosote on the ties. It was filtering through our skin. Rich advised us to wear leather gloves, and keep away from liquor and women.

Sometimes we laid steel. This was tougher than laying ties. Eight men with tongs, four on each end, wrastled a length of steel rail. If one of the eight stumbled it meant down with the rail.

Ed Bass, a lanky young farmer of the region, who was trying to dodge starvation by a summer on the section, had his foot crushed that way. He lay on his back and cursed the gang till you'd think his mouth would blister. We put him on a handcar, and Tony and I had to pump him back to the village. He cursed us two all the way, and called us "lousy Wops." Tony wanted to kick him, but though the lousy Ku Kluxer deserved a kicking, I stopped Tony.

There were twenty-four of us on Section Gang 10. And we spoke six languages, and feared and suspected each other like good patriots. There were five Wops, three Hunyaks, a Swede, a Jew, an Irishman (there's always one apiece for every kind of excitement in the world), three Mexicans, two Poles, and a bunch of Yank hundred-percenters. There was also a Negro named Harry.

On a Section Gang

We sweated every day under the same sun; we slept in the same crummy bunkhouse and ate the same commissary garbage. But we hated each other, and felt superior to each other. Such is the Adamic curse that has been laid on the American labor movement.

Every one hated Rich the Foreman. That was one principle on which we all could agree. I can't understand dicks, cops, hangmen, professional gunmen, or men like Rich. You have to look upon them as pathological specimens. I guess most men go crazy when they are turned loose with a club, and told to go the limit.

Rich went the limit. He was a big Yank about forty, with one of those stern Indian faces some Americans have. He looked like a Texan. He had those blue unflinching eyes of the eagle and killer. He never laughed. He was powerful enough to lick any one on the gang, and we knew it. He was always pushing us on. He was a fanatic. God, the passion, the fury, the religious fire that man put into bossing a section! I am sure it was eating him up. And he was doing it all for $96 a month. Can you understand these mysteries of human character?

In the mornings, we pumped our handcars seven miles or more to the job. Rich stood erect on the first car, like Washington crossing the Delaware. The night fogs still clung to the sides of the hills. His keen eyes roamed about, his ears listened. Suddenly he blew his whistle, and we jumped like mad and lifted the heavy cars off the rails just in time. An express train thundered by a second later, the children and ladies waving gayly at us.

Section gangs were sometimes devoured by these thunderbolts. Rich saved us from death several times. He carried quite a responsibility.

He hated to see any one stop to light a pipe, or take a drink, or anything. He watched you with a suspicious glare, and without saying anything, made you feel guilty as hell.

Once Joe, the water-boy, a Wop kid, thought he saw a snake by the side of the track. Rich's back was turned, so the kid picked up a rock and chased the snake. He wandered into the bushes and was gone about five minutes. Meanwhile some one started yelling, "Water Boy! Water Boy!" but Joe wasn't in sight. Others began yelling, just to be mean. It was their way of annoying Rich—to show him they had no rights on the gang, not even a good water-boy.

Rich swelled up with wrath like a poisoned pup. He began yelling and cursing, and then Joe appeared grinning, with some flowers in his hand. He had missed the snake, but found some pretty flowers. Rich went over to him, grabbed his arm and twisted it behind his back until the kid screamed for mercy.

Tony, an old Italian laborer, muttered something in Italian. Rich let up on the kid and turned on Tony and blistered him with curses. And cursed the whole gang, and asked us what we were loafing around for that way.

On a Section Gang

One day in July was the hottest day I have known in my life. You could see the heat waves steaming from the ties. The rails were redhot like a frying pan. We rushed Joe off his feet, getting us buckets of drinking water.

It was almost noon, when suddenly something happened. Swen, a big good-natured Swede, was holding the spike while Harry sledged it into place. Suddenly Swen toppled over, and Harry's sledge missed his skull by a half-inch.

The sun had knocked Swen out. We got him under a tree, and sloshed him with water. He was unconscious and breathing hard. After a while he came to. All the time we were working over him Rich was trying to tell us to get back to work. But every one pretended to be busy with Swen, and quite deaf.

Finally Rich began roaring at us. "Get to hell back on the job, or I'll knock hell outa some of yeh, yeh bunch of bastards!" We were all lying about under the tree, resting, and no one made a move to get up.

"It's too hot, Meesta Reech," said Tony, the old wop. "Yep, Rich, it's too hot," others muttered, as Rich went down the line. It was a kind of strike, the first time anything like it had happened in Rich's experience, I guess.

He was dumbfounded, but kept his wits. He saw the gang was united on something at last, and had him licked. So he broke us up by going after individuals.

"Here, Stubby," he said, "you don't think it's

too hot, do you? Get back to work there, Stubby."

Stubby was a glum old Yank about sixty-one. You could see he was ashamed of himself as he rose slowly and hobbled back on the track. For the next half-hour he shoveled ballast all by himself in the redhot sun while we watched him and sneered.

I never saw a strike yet where the Yanks were not the first to scab.

At last, one by one, we all drifted back to the track, and worked in a bath of salt sweat.

I liked Old Tony. He was one of those hard round-shouldered little Italians with wrinkled walnut faces who can survive anything. Their people have been peasants since Julius Cæsar, and they are as simple and natural as a good dog. You get to love them the same way.

Tony had a little garden by the box cars where we bunked. He raised a few geraniums and scallions there, and had a great time.

One of the Poles had an accordion. He and the other Poles would sometimes sing and play on the bunkhouse steps in the evening. This was generally after pay day, while they still had money for liquor. The moon shone down, the katydids buzzsawed in the grass. The Poles played the accordion and looked at the moon.

Gandy dancers are the lowest in the scale of migratory workers. The younger stiffs won't touch a section job if they can help it. The pay is too low, and the conditions impossible. That's why you find so many older men on the section gangs, and so many foreigners. And that's why no American labor union has ever bothered much with organizing the gandy dancers. I guess they're too low.

Harry and Bill were playing casino at the table. Joe the water-boy was reading a cowboy magazine near the lamp. Swen was snoring like a hog in his bunk. Sevelod was still washing his Sunday shirt. Through the side door you could see the night, the big black sky and the lonesome trees. I played on the harmonica.

We were the only ones in our car who hadn't gone down to the village to spend our two weeks' pay. About nine o'clock there was a lot of laughing outside, and the Williams brothers burst in.

They were farm boys of the region who were working on the section that summer, because farming was bad. They were the kind of lanky, sour, gloomy Yanks who can only be happy when they are violently drunk.

"We come back to get the rest of our pay," Elmer yelled. "Why don't you guys come down the village? It's a big night."

"Yop, a lot of the miners are out, and there's a big crap game in Jones's barn," said Fred.

Elmer was rummaging in his bunk, and found his money. Also he was putting on a necktie, and smiling. Fred pulled the necktie off his neck.

"That ain't fair," he yelled. "Cripes, he's dollin' up! That ain't fair!"

"You put on your own necktie," Elmer said, "that'll make it fair."

"The hell I will," said Fred, "we'll see who makes her without no necktie."

Fred explained drunkenly to us that there was a new girl at Carney's speakeasy-hotel and all the boys were after her. Fred and Elmer were going to compete which would win her for the night.

They went out whooping and cursing.

They staggered back at three in the morning, when we were all rolled in our bunks, sleeping.

Fred had a handkerchief tied around his head, through which great gobs of blood showed. Elmer supported him, and pleaded with him in a tearful drunken voice: "Honest, Fred, I didn't mean to hit yuh so hard. You're my own brother, Fred, and any one goes to the mat with you, goes to the mat with me, see?"

"But you shouldn't have done it, Elmer, not to your own brother, god damn it," Fred said, tearfully, as he flopped to the floor.

Elmer picked him up and began undressing him.

"I don't know how I happened to get that chair in my hand, honest, Fred, god damn it, would I hit my own brother that way with a chair? Now lay down and take it easy, Fred."

They kept it up until dawn, arguing and pleading, and then we all arose and had breakfast. Fred and Elmer were pale and glum, but they kept up their end gamely that day on the section gang.

LOVE ON A GARBAGE DUMP

CERTAIN enemies have spread the slander that I once attended Harvard college. This is a lie. I worked on the garbage dump in Boston, city of Harvard. But that's all.

The Boston dump is a few miles out of town, on an estuary of the harbor. Imagine a plain 200 acres square, containing no trees or houses, but blasted and nightmarish like a drawing by Doré, a land of slime and mud, a purgatory.

Hills of rotten fish dot this plain; there are also mountains of rusty tomato cans. The valleys are strewn with weird gardens of manycolored rags, of bottles, cracked mirrors, newspapers, and pillboxes.

Garbage gives off smoke as it decays, also melancholy smells like a zoo. The pervading smoke and odor of the dump made me feel at first as if all America had ended, and was rotting into death. Buzzards lounged in the sky, or hopped about, pecking clumsily at the nation's corpse.

I was young and violent then, and must confess this image of America's extinction filled me with Utopian dreams.

Working on the dump were 30 men, women and pale children. Unfortunate peasants of Italy and

Portugal, they sat in sleet and wind on each side of a conveyor.

This moving belt was an endless cornucopia of refuse. As it creaked past them the peasants snatched like magpies at odds and ends of salvage. Bits of machinery, and wearing apparel, rubber goods, etc., were rescued from the general corruption.

Later the Salvation Army and other profiteering ghouls received this salvaged ordure, and re-sold it to the poorest poor.

I will not be picturesque, and describe the fantastic objects that turned up during a day on this conveyor.

Nor will I tell how the peasants whimsically decorated themselves with neckties, alarm clocks, ribbons, and enema bags, mantillas and other strange objects, so that by the evening some of them resembled futurist Christmas trees.

It was their mode of humor. As I have said, I was too young and violent then to appreciate such humor.

Seeing them at their masquerade, I was sometimes sickened, as if corpses on a battlefield were to rise and dance to patriotic jazz.

I worked in the paper baling press.

Two Italians stood on a Niagara of old newspapers, and shoveled down newspapers to another worker and myself.

We distributed the tons of newspapers inside a

great box eight feet tall. When the box was full, we packed it tight by means of an immense wooden lever from which we hung by our arms. Then we roped up the bales, and wagons hauled them to the boiling vats.

Shoveling newspapers all day, jumping on them, kicking them, was not an unpleasant job for one who hated capitalism.

When my muscles ached I would sometimes rest, and pore over muddy scraps of newspaper.

As I meditated on the advice to the lovelorn section, or the bon mots of famous columnists, or as I studied the Broadway theater gossip, and the latest news of disarmament, my anger would rise and choke me.

Then I would be glad my job enabled me to trample on these newspapers, to spit upon them, and to shovel them contemptuously into great bales meant for the boiling vat.

My working partner was a dark, gloomy man of about 50, with queer black eyes, a saffron face, and a hawk nose. I thought he was an Italian immigrant, and could speak no English. For the first three months we exchanged no word of conversation, but grunted side by side like truck horses in harness.

One day as I cursed at the newspapers, he muttered in slow but accurate English:

"I would like to kill all them."

"Who?" I asked.

"The editors of garbage," he said, and bent again to his shovel.

So we became friends. After that my days were filled with discussions with this man on the horrors of American civilization.

He was not an Italian, but a Crow Indian, and his white man's name was James Cherry. It is unusual to find an Indian in the eastern cities, but there are a few.

Cherry's story was an odd one. He had been born on a reservation in Montana, and had attended the Carlisle Indian College maintained by the government.

This James Cherry had been gifted with a mind. But the U. S. government has never admitted that Indians have minds. At Carlisle the young students are taught only manual trades. This was Cherry's chief grievance.

James Cherry had graduated as a carpenter, with a hatred of the white government that denied him a real education. After years of brooding his hate turned into a mania. He became firmly convinced that he was a great inventor, who was on the way to inventing a death-ray machine that would kill all the white tyrants.

Cherry had an enormous craving for wholesale murder, he longed for the day when his machine would be perfect enough to wipe out by secret and terrifying means, whole regiments of congressmen, bankers, college presidents, automobile manufacturers and authors.

I tried to point out to him that this would be of no avail, that other capitalists would rise to take their places. I quoted Marx to this madman, to prove to him our remedy lay in changing the economic system that produced such men. Only by organizing the working class for a final assault on the system could anything be accomplished, I argued.

But he was a fanatic individualist, and our debates were long, furious and without avail.

As well quote Marx to Coolidge as to this Indian whose powerful mind had coiled in upon itself, like a snake in the throes of suicide.

I am always sorry for these mental freaks one meets among the workers. There are many of them. It is the result of the ferocious ideals that are taught them in public school. They are urged to aspire to the Presidency of the United States, they are enabled to read and write, and then, with this dangerous combination of Napoleonic ambition and kindergarten learning, they are shot into factories, mills and mines, to be hopeless wage slaves for life.

Well balanced intellectuals among the workers become revolutionists. The others become freaks and madmen.

Bill Sheehan, my sailor friend, who is a connoisseur of such types, once told me of an elderly dishwasher he knew. This man was obsessed with the idea that he was a great orchestral leader.

Every night he would lock himself into his hall bedroom in a cheap rooming house, and turn on a Victrola. Then, with a baton, for hours, he would passionately conduct symphonies and operas. If anything displeased him, he would stop the phonograph, and in stern accents order his orchestra to go back to a certain passage. They did so, of course. These rehearsals went on for fifteen years.

Bill Sheehan also told me of a shipmate, a giant stoker who went on a long drunk in Yokohama, and staggered back in two days with a large butterfly tattooed on his forehead. He had had it done while drunk. He was a serious person and so humiliated by this folly, now permanent like the brand of Cain, that he grew morbid and read books and eventually became a Theosophist.

I was 19 years old, and a fool, and in love with two women. One was Concha, a Portuguese girl who worked on the garbage dump, and the other was a New England aristocrat who lived on Beacon Hill.

I had never seen the latter, nor did I even know her name. To reach the street car from the fat Armenian's rooming house where I lived, I had to pass along a certain street on Beacon Hill. At night, returning, rankly odorous and sweaty from work, I passed the same street.

From the window of a beautiful old colonial home on this street, a girl played Mozart in the dusk. I would linger there and listen with a beautiful confused aching in my "soul."

Behind the yellow shades, I could see in candlelight the girl's silhouette as she sat at the piano.

That's all, but I was madly in love with her.

I believed then in two opposing kinds of love, the physical and the spiritual, and that one was base, and the other noble.

Concha, I knew definitely to my shame, I wanted physically. I had heard a Portuguese worker boast he had gone home with her often and stopped with her. This, in my loneliness, inflamed me, and I wanted her, too.

She spoke little English. She was 18, swarthy, tall and vital, as handsome as a wildcat. Life burned in her full breasts, and radiated from her rounded hips, legs, arms. She had too much life, and could not contain it all. She danced, joked, sang, her eyes sparkled, she was full of dangerous electricity. Concha had not yet been beaten by the gray years poverty brings the worker. She was the crazy young clown and melodious lark of our garbage dump.

She seemed to like me. All the men flirted with her, and Juan, the boastful young Portuguese, was considered her favored suitor. But at lunch time, she let me take her behind the tomato can mountain, and kiss her. This happened many days. It thrilled me with adolescent joy and pride.

One day I asked her to let me come to her home sometimes like Juan. She smiled mysteriously, and patted her gorgeous blue-black hair.

"Maybe yes," she said. "Bimeby, you see it."

Juan grew jealous of me, and I was jealous of him. Once he caught me with Concha behind the tomato cans, and scowled at us and plucked his fierce black mustache.

"Sonofagun!" he said to me. "You take my girl, huh!"

"Ah, go to hell," I said, bravely drunk with "physical" love.

The whistle blew just then, and Juan walked sullenly back to work. Concha laughed as if she had enjoyed the joke.

"Juan, he crazy man!" she whispered. "No good man, you come any way bimeby to my house, next week, maybe?"

I cannot tell how marvelous this seemed to me, in my adolescent fever. Concha loved me, evidently. She preferred me to all the other men on the garbage dump. I could not sleep nights thinking about my beautiful Concha. I could scarcely wait.

It was quitting time, and I was stripping off my overalls behind the paper press, when James Cherry, glaring about him to make sure no one was listening, confided to me another of his strange, dismal secrets.

"I have just invented a new machine!" he said, his black eyes burning holes in my face. "Listen, this time it is the radio-eye machine! The scientists have been hunting for it, but I have found it! I can turn it on, and penetrate into any house, see everything that is happening all over the world."

"Can you see Queen Mary taking her bath?" I asked casually, to show some interest.

"Certainly, but that is nothing, it is trivial," he whispered. "I can see the Wall street bankers at their plots. I can see the government stealing the land from the Indians. I can see the white men who murder Negroes. I will bring them to trial! I will tell the truth to every one!"

"That's fine, Cherry," I said, "keep it up!" I shook his hand and left him among the tons of soiled newspapers, sunk in his Olympian fantasies. In ancient times the madmen among the poor dreamed of revenging their wrongs through God; now they dream in machines.

I hurried home, and washed up. Then I ate at my beanery, and walked slowly toward the North End, sunk in fantasies as crazy as James Cherry's, perhaps, but more exquisite.

That noon, behind the tomato cans, Concha had smiled quietly, and said: "To-night maybe you come by my house." She gave me the address scrawled in a pathetic childish hand on an envelope flap. Now I was on my way there.

It was spring, I was 19 years old, and on the road to my beloved. Every nerve quivered with a foolish delight. I can never forget this all.

She lived in one of those wooden tenement shacks in the North End, near the tavern where Paul Revere mounted for his famous revolutionary ride.

She greeted me at the door with a shy little smile. The rooms were low-ceilinged, stuffy and lit by a kerosene lamp. They were exactly as they must have been in 1850—no modern improvements. An old woman and two children stared dully at me.

"My mamma, my brodder, my seesta," said Concha, pointing her hand at them. The old woman looked like a Rembrandt painting in the lamplight. She was wrinkled and sad, and kept staring at me vacantly. The children had Concha's Latin beauty, but were pale and undernourished, and dressed in rags.

And so we sat and stared at each other in gloomy silence. I was embarrassed, and wondered what would happen next.

"Luis! Trinidad!" the old woman spoke sharply to the children, coming out of her stupor at last. They rose and followed her meekly into the bedroom. They shut the door.

Concha smiled then, and came over and sat on my lap.

My heart beat fast, and as I breathed the warm life-smell of her vital body, I felt a shock of joy.

She had decorated herself for my coming. She had rouged her cheeks, and hung pendants from her ears. I was sure she had found them on the garbage dump. The purple silk waist she wore I was also sure came from the dump, and the faded linen tablecloth, and the chromo pictures on the wall.

"You like-a me, boy?" Concha whispered, her burning lips at my ear.

"Yes," I said.

"Me like-a you, too," she said.

We kissed. A long time passed. I could hear the old mother and the children climbing into a creaky bed in the bedroom.

"You gimme dollar, maybe?" Concha said.

"What?"

Love on a Garbage Dump

I was startled.

"Maybe you gimme dollar," Concha repeated painfully. She saw the shocked look on my face, and it hurt her. She began talking very rapidly, earnestly, painfully.

"Me poor. Me make $8 a week. Me pappa he die. Me pappa he sick and die. Me mamma she sick. Me like-a you, no bad girl. Me send brodder, seesta, to the American school-a. Me too much poor. Sabe?"

There was an ache around my heart as I gave her the dollar.

I walked home slowly, heavy with a load of shame. Physical love had betrayed me again. I walked through Boston streets, glamorous with May, and darkness, and lights and sounds, and cursed myself, and cursed my evil doggy nature.

It had all ended in cheapness. She had done it just for the dollar, not for love, my proud wildcat beauty! My God, would I ever escape from the garbage dump of America!

Almost automatically, my feet led me to the street on aristocratic Beacon Hill. The other girl was still playing Mozart from the window. I leaned against a railing, and listened to the pure, bright flow with a breaking heart. What a contrast!

This was the world of spiritual beauty, of music, and art, and ethereal love, and I, the proletarian, could never enter it. My destiny was evident; I would die like a stinking old dog on a garbage dump.

I wanted to cry for yearning and self-pity. I was ready to give up the endless futile struggle for a living. I grew weak and cowardly, and wanted to die.

And then a policeman broke this evil spell. He loomed up out of the mysterious spring night, and poked me in the ribs with his club.

"Move on, bum," he said, "bums have got no business hanging around this part of town."

Of course I moved on. Anger boiled up in me, anger to save me from mushy self-pity, harsh, clean anger like the gales at sea.

As I walked along the Esplanade by the Charles River, everything straightened itself out again in my head, and I came back to the strong proletarian realities.

"Mozart and candlelight and the spiritual values, to hell with you all!" I thought. "You are parasites. Concha is the one who pays for you! It's more honorable to work on a garbage dump than to be a soulful parasite on Beacon Hill.

"If Concha needed a dollar, she had a right to ask for it! It is that lazy, useless parasite who plays Mozart who forced Concha so low!" Then, unlike James Cherry, I dreamed angrily of a great movement to set the working-class free. I walked home in double-quick time, in my fantasy a young Communist marching to the barricades.

FASTER, AMERICA, FASTER!

The private train never stopped. It was like war. It smashed the peace of the dark American fields. Frogs leaped into the marsh-pools as the monster passed. Birds waked and screamed. Trees bent before the storm. The blow struck the still farmhouses, and they trembled in every rafter. Fever. No more quiet. The moon reeled. The virgin night was raped from dreams. Speed! The private train never stopped. There were two luxury cars and a locomotive.

The private train never stopped. Its whistle and bell banged and boasted: The world is mine! They clanged: Get out of the way! The Big Boss is coming! The private train spat golden sparks into the humble face of Night. It was destined for Hollywood. Erwin Schmidt, the German-American movie millionaire, had chartered it for his youngest star and some friends. The boilers bellowed. The rails shrieked like dying women. Loafers at small country towns were grazed by a thunderbolt of flying steel and steam. They saw a shower of golden windows. Cities and towns roared by. Mountains raced up and down, see-sawed. The private train never stopped. It had the right of way from Atlantic to Pacific. It owned the American horizon. (America is a private train crashing over the slippery rails of

History. Faster, faster, America!) The private train never stopped.

In a huge, wonderful armchair Mr. Schmidt leaned back and smiled. He was forty-five years old, and bald, pink, shining and perfect. He was very tolerant. He was sure. He pressed a button and the world entered with a tray, and brought him what he wished. He was a sophisticated Menckenite and connoisseur.

My dear, he said in a fatherly voice, to the raw little flapper opposite him, let me ask George to fill your glass again.

Oh, thank you, Mr. Schmidt, she stammered nervously, licking her dry lips and smiling.

My dear child, he cooed, you mustn't call me Mr. Schmidt! Mr. Schmidt indeed! So formal, aren't you? All my little girls call me Pops. Just Pops.

Yes, Pops.

That's better, Angel-Face.

George, the tall Negro in white, entered with low, dramatic, oriental bowings and ceremony. He poured, with perfect art, wine into two thin glasses. He dimmed the lights in the Czarist stateroom being whirled eighty miles an hour through the ancient, humble night.

My, my, Dot, now you're a real star. Yes, at seventeen your name will be blazing in electric lights on the theaters of every city in the world. Isn't that wonderful? Yesterday a mere stenographer, tomorrow a world figure, like Gloria Swanson or Valentino, no less. Don't it thrill you, my little Cinderella?

Oh, it certainly does, Mr—Pops.

She had baby blue eyes, soft as a mongrel's. Blonde, wavy bob. Pink and white enamel face, beautiful as a flat magazine cover done by a Hearst artist. Just out of high school, and bewildered. Her little heart was beating. Her little brain was puzzled. What did Pops want?

In the next car, a long room decorated in gilt like the Czar's palace, a male press agent, three female movie actresses, a female scenario writer, two male movie executives, and a male British novelist were drinking and dancing to the radio. None of them needed monkey glands.

Gladys La Svelte tossed off a bumper of champagne, bit the neck of the stately British author, and wanted to pull the engine cord.

Henry, a short Negro in white, uttered, with oriental bowings and humility: Please, ma'am, that cord is for emergencies only.

Let's pull it anyway. I want the train to go faster. I want speed—speed—speed.

Please, ma'am—

Speed. Faster, faster! Tell the engineer, faster, faster!

Yes, ma'am.

She didn't pull it. The radio brought the history of science to a grand climax. It transmitted *Yes Sir, That's My Baby* from Chicago. The jazz band at the Hotel Karnac was ya-hooing like mad.

It positively gets into one's blood, said the British

novelist naïvely. What a country, what a country! Faster, faster, he chortled.

He thought of his marvelous Hollywood contract, and bit the neck of Gladys La Svelte to show his joy. He unbent. This was a riotous surprise to every one, and they whacked him with colored toy balloons.

The fireman was shoveling coal into the fiery furnace. He was a haggard young American roughneck. He had been in three wrecks, and in one of them a piece of iron entered his skull.

She's going good now, ain't she? he yelled belligerently, his hard face set, as he wiped his smutty brow with a hunk of cotton waste.

Too good, said the old engineer with a sour sneer. He was disillusioned with speed; had driven express trains for forty years. But Mr. Schmidt had promised him fifty dollars at the end of his run.

Whatddye mean, too good? Ain't I givin' yuh all the steam yuh need? yelled the fireman.

The engineer couldn't hear and didn't answer. He was worrying. The fireman repeated the question belligerently. His nerves were on edge. His girl had thrown him down and had married a salesman. The fireman had been on an awful bootleg jag for three days. He was a hard, bitter drinker since that last wreck, when he was knocked on the head. But the engineer was worrying.

I must watch out. There's always a jam near Des Moines. Jim Moore got wrecked there only last month, with a clear track, too. And these specials ball up the schedule. I must watch out. Jim was wrecked. He took the hill, whistling, and there was Number 4 staring him right in the face. I must watch out.

Faster, faster, yelled the fireman. You got all the steam she can stand, ain't yuh? He was mad with rage for some reason, and slammed the coal like a furious devil into the firebox. Faster, faster, you old bastard.

The engineer was startled. Was it me you called that? he shouted, staring down with stern eyes.

Yeh, you, the fireman roared, shaking his shovel at the engineer. You, you, you. His hair streamed in the gale, and the black and yellow glare of the furnace illuminated him with the fires of hell.

In the narrow pantry, George and Henry, the Negroes in white, drooped wearily like heartsick mothers at a bedside.

Ain't they awful?

Yop, plumb coo-coo.

I wish I could get some sleep.

No sleep on this trip, Big Boy.

Honest, it ain't worth even the big tips. I hate to serve them.

Last time for me, I'll tell the world.

There's that bell again. Hope the old ofay busts a blood vessel or something.

Slip a white powder in his gin.

Wish I had the nerve.

Then suddenly oriental, George purringly poured for Mr. Schmidt the finest wine money could buy, into the finest glasses money could buy.

Just turn those other lights out, too, said the magnate. They hurt my eyes.

Yes, sir. Yes, sir.

The private train never stopped.

They were Hollywooding in the next car. They were wasting life. They screamed, wrestled, frazzled, mushed, rubbed, gooed and ate huge chicken and bacon sandwiches. An executive and an actress stole off into a stateroom. The others petted, laughed, screamed, gobbled. They smeared mustard on each other. A dress was torn. The floor was cluttered with napkins, salad dressing, corks and cigarette butts. The radio yammered. The night flew by. Through the windows all the dark farmhouses, trees, rivers, flashed by like a cheap movie. The dark, old American fields roared with a mighty voice. There was a protest against this new thing. But the private train never stopped.

Haw, haw, let's serenade Dot and Pops.

No, let's tell the engineer to go faster, shrieked Gladys.

Some one stuck his head out of the window. Fast enough for me. Fast as a Keystone comedy.

Aw, come on, let's serenade Dot and Pops. He's our host, ain't he? Gotta show our 'preciation, ain't we?

The fireman slammed open the firebox door. He bellowed with delight when the tiger-blast struck his sweaty face. His muscles bulged. His chest gleamed. He danced like a clumsy bull. He

Faster, America, Faster!

climbed up the cab. The old engineer screamed. He hit the old engineer over the skull with his shovel. The engineer died. The fireman danced.

Faster, faster, the fireman screamed, flinging his giant arms to the gale. Faster when I tell yuh to go faster. I'm boss here now. I'm a millionaire. I'm King of the World!

The private train never stopped. It leaped ahead as if a giant had kicked it forward.

Mr. Schmidt was slightly sweating.

I could get any girl I wanted in the world. But I want only you, my bonny daisy.

Oh, Pops, you do say such pretty things. You talk like a poet.

Little rabbit, you're first beginning to know me. People think I'm a cold, dull business man, but I have an artist's soul. That is really the secret of my success. I'll make a great artist out of you before I'm through with you. If it costs me a cool million.

Oh, Pops! You make me so happy.

Kiss me, Dottie.

I'm so young, she lisped coyly, I don't know about these things. Isn't it wrong, Pops?

Henry and George were badly frightened. They stuck their heads out of the pantry window. The wind smote them like an uppercut from Jack Dempsey's fist.

Gawd, she'll jump the track at this rate, sure. I never saw a train act this way.

I guess it's all right, George. I guess so. Old

Gordon's driving her, and he knows what he's doing.
I guess so.

It don't feel right, I tell yuh. No. Too fast, too
fast!

Old Gordon's running her. Guess so. Guess so.
It's all right, George. Guess so. Guess so, one
Negro waiter said to the other.

The gaudy mob poured in to serenade Pops. But
the stateroom door was locked against them. They
pounded on the door with bottles and yelled Hey!
Hey! They rocked on their feet. The private train
was shimmying like mad. It never stopped. A few
were sick. Gladys La Svelte vomited on the Czarist
floor. Every one laughed like a zoo. Britain supported America and held her head down.

Gladys grew histrionic. She wept like Jesus. He's
double-crossed me, she screamed, and broke away.
She kicked at the door crazily. I know what's going
on in there. He's thrown me over for that little
Kewpie doll, the old cradle-snatcher. But I'll show
him. I'll tell the newspapers he's crazy for young
girls. I'll break him. I'll sue him. He dragged me
down.

The others laughed like a zoo. They rocked and
shimmied with the train. Aw, forget it, Gladys.
Come on and sing, Gladys. Be a sport. He's our
host, ain't he? The British novelist used his monocle
haughtily, and thought of his contract. Gladys was
vulgar. But there was laughter of coyotes and peacocks. Every one burst into song. Hail, hail, the
gang's all here, so what the hell do—

Faster, America, Faster!

Henry and George rushed in with immense eyes and pork-pale faces.

Too fast—too fast, they stammered—

Laughter like a zoo. They bladdered the Negroes with toy balloons.

Then—OUT!

Life exploded like a bomb.

Then—POW!

The world shot from a cannon in flame. Coney Island fireworks. Crucifix pain.

Tidal wave, earthquake, last lonely screams of little children eaten by a giant. Snap and crack. Fade out. Then quiet. A bird sang in the sudden sweet gloom. There was a smell of roasted flesh.

The great monster lay on its side, tons of steel writhing like a snake. Huge steam-clouds hissed from the dragon's wounds. The old countryside was cool, dark and still. Yes, a bird sang.

Mr. Schmidt's pampered guts lay neglected in the ballast. The last white stars shone in the sky. Gladys was grinning with some bloody joke. She was red and nude. The British novelist was undignified; he had no arms. Negro George was long, flat and patient. The night was very dark and sweet. Little Dot hugged the grass by the track. The fireman's wild head had rolled away. There was the smell of flesh. A bird sang. The press agent's belly was like an open mouth.

Faster, faster.

Revolution.

A pale farmer came running from the dark. He

had a sickle in his hand. A pale worker in overalls came up, with a hammer. They soberly began the rescue work. Dawn grew. The red morning star appeared.

America is a private train rushing to Hollywood.

Faster, faster, America!

A STRANGE FUNERAL IN BRADDOCK

Listen to the mournful drums of a strange funeral.
Listen to the story of a strange American funeral.

In the town of Braddock, Pennsylvania,
Where steel-mills live like foul dragons, burning, devouring man and earth and sky,
It is spring. Now the spring has wandered in, a frightened child in the land of the steel ogres,
And Jan Clepak, the great grinning Bohemian, on his way to work at six in the morning,
Sees buttons of bright grass on the hills across the river, and plum-trees hung with wild white blossoms,
And as he sweats half-naked at his pudding trough, a fiend by the lake of brimstone,
The plum-trees soften his heart,
The green grass-memories return and soften his heart,
And he forgets to be hard as steel and remembers only his wife's breasts, his baby's little laughters and the way men sing when they are drunk and happy,
He remembers cows and sheep, and the grinning peasants, and the villages and fields of sunny Bohemia.

Listen to the mournful drums of a strange funeral.
Listen to the story of a strange American funeral.

Wake up, wake up! Jan Clepak, the furnaces are roaring like tigers,
The flames are flinging themselves at the high roof, like mad, yellow tigers at their cage,
Wake up! it is ten o'clock, and the next batch of mad, flowing steel is to be poured into your puddling trough,
Wake up! wake up! for a flawed lever is cracking in one of those fiendish cauldrons,
Wake up! and wake up! for now the lever has cracked, and the steel is raging and running down the floor like an escaped madman,
Wake up! Oh, the dream is ended, and the steel has swallowed you forever, Jan Clepak!

Listen to the mournful drums of a strange funeral.
Listen to the story of a strange American funeral.

Now three tons of hard steel hold at their heart the bones, flesh, nerves, the muscles, brains and heart of Jan Clepak,
They hold the memories of green grass and sheep, the plum-trees, the baby-laughter, and the sunny Bohemian villages.
And the directors of the steel-mill present the great coffin of steel and man-memories to the widow of Jan Clepak,
And on a great truck it is borne now to the great trench in the graveyard,
And Jan Clepak's widow and two friends ride in a carriage behind the block of steel that holds Jan Clepak,

A Strange Funeral in Braddock

And they weep behind the carriage blinds, and mourn the soft man who was slain by hard steel.

Listen to the mournful drums of a strange funeral.
Listen to the story of a strange American funeral.

Now three thinkers are thinking strange thoughts in the graveyard.
"O, I'll get drunk and stay drunk forever, I'll never marry woman, or father laughing children,
I'll forget everything, I'll be nothing from now on,
Life is a dirty joke, like Jan's funeral!"
One of the friends is thinking in the sweet-smelling graveyard,
As a derrick lowers the three tons of steel that held Jan Clepak.
(LISTEN TO THE DRUMS OF THE STRANGE AMERICAN FUNERAL!)

"I'll wash clothes, I'll scrub floors, I'll be a fifty-cent whore, but my children will never work in the steel-mill!"
Jan Clepak's wife is thinking as earth is shoveled over the great steel coffin,
In the spring sunlight, in the soft April air,
(LISTEN TO THE DRUMS OF THE STRANGE AMERICAN FUNERAL!)

"I'll make myself hard as steel, harder,
I'll come some day and make bullets of Jan's body, and shoot them into a tyrant's heart!"

The other friend is thinking, the listener,
He who listened to the mournful drums of the strange funeral,
Who listened to the story of the strange American funeral,
And turned as mad as a fiendish cauldron with cracked lever.

LISTEN TO THE MOURNFUL DRUMS OF A STRANGE FUNERAL.
LISTEN TO THE STORY OF A STRANGE AMERICAN FUNERAL.

BIG JOE'S BIRTHDAY

Others got tired, others lost hope and shut their mouths, or started little garages and grocery stores, found harbors of peace,

Others sold out, turned respectable labor leader, or politician or foreman,

But Big Joe never shut his mouth, or turned respectable.

He stuck; the enemy nailed him to a hundred crosses, they strangled him in a hundred prisons,

They spattered his body and soul with their machine-gun fire of lies, beatings and persecutions,

His quieter friends thought Joe was wasting his life, his wife grew discouraged, his children became Americanized and left him,

But Big Joe Connolly could never desert the labor movement,

The cords of birth still held him to his mother.

They tried to make a foreman of him once, but he turned them down,

And once a silly District Attorney tried to buy Joe, but Joe laughed at him in the prison.

And once they tried to frame him up with a woman, but he laughed at the woman.

And once they tried to lynch him, they strung him up and let him down, but they never made him show the yellow,

The cords of birth still bound him to his mother.

He never knew why he was loyal or why he would
    rather die than desert the labor movement.
And thinkers would argue with him, and try to
    understand his passion, but he could not explain
    it to them.
He could not explain that his mother had given him
    birth on the stormy sea of poverty,
Where strong men had wept, knowing the bitter
    fate before the child,
But his mother's faith shone like a light on a rock,
And she bred him to manhood, despite the black mid-
    nights and steep waves of poverty,
And the cords of birth still bound him to his mother.

In darkest city tenements she bred him.
The sun was quenched there, and failure lived in each
    room,
And landlords and bosses guarded the prison; there
    was no escape.
But the gas-lit dungeons throbbed with his mother's
    fierce chant,
"The Poor must not die! The Poor must live and be
    brave!"
So the cords of birth ever bound him to his mother.

Her back was twisted and bent with many loads, her
    hands scarred by a thousand labors.
She was small, weak, kind, but dark and terrible as a
    jaguar at times.
She sewed, swept, cooked, she never rested,
She took in washing, she stole wood and coal from
    the railroad yards in winter,

Big Joe's Birthday

When her man was killed, she did not despair, but went on fighting,
And Big Joe loved her, and never forgot her after she died.
The years went by, jail-sentences, discords, strikes, defeats, spies, thirty-five years of tragedy and hope in the labor movement,
And the cords of birth still bound him to his mother.

Big Joe Connolly is fifty years old to-day.
And it is thirty-five years since he entered the labor movement.
And the workers have brought a horseshoe of blood-red roses to the union hall,
And they present it to Joe, who blushes behind his big gray mustache like a school-boy,
And they shake his hand, punching him and hugging him like huge brother-bears, showing him their rough love,
The pretty young girls kiss him, and the big, slow, kind mothers in shawls smile as they clasp his hand,
The children climb his knees and grab his arms for affection,
And some one makes a rough speech, built of honest words like bricks,
And Joe answers in a torrent of words like logs pouring down a Maine river,
And the workers listen with tears in their eyes, glad that he will be loyal to the grave,
And glad that the cords of birth still bind him to his mother.

THIRD DEGREE

Five strong detectives are in a cell with a prisoner,
And by God, they know they will make him speak!
They push against each other blindly, like mad, thirsty bulls pent in a cattle car,
They are anxious, there is not enough room for them in the dark cell,
Their heavy suits hamper them, their white collars choke them,
They grunt and sweat and curse as their blackjacks rise and fall,
Five strong detectives in a cell with a prisoner.

They have eagerly twisted the arms of the prisoner behind him until the bones cracked.
They have battered his pale temples with their blackjacks and kicked in his fourth rib.
They have walked on his spine, and beat his mouth to a bloody pulp.
They have blackened his eyes, and flattened his nose.
The five strong detectives in a cell with a prisoner,
And by God, they will surely make him speak.

The moon, like a white innocent, blunders in, and then vanishes, knowing she's not wanted.
A taxi-cab rolls by in the street above, with a drunken girl laughing to her man.
And a guard rattles his keys down the corridor, and the gas-jet whistles a lonely little tune,

Third Degree

And prisoners in the prison turn on their cots and
   dream they are home again,
While the five strong detectives argue in the cell
   with the prisoner,
Telling him, by God, he must speak.

Oh, lead blackjacks plead with the prisoner to speak,
   and hard shoes, and hairy Judas-knuckles.
And his pounding heart shouts that he must speak.
And his bleeding body weeps like a baby gnawed by
   a rat, Speak!
And his brain bursts with agony and screams, Speak,
   Speak!
And his blood moans: "Your woman waits for you, if
   you will only speak."
And the whole world roars with a million wild voices
   in his ears, O Jesus, man! Speak!
But the prisoner will not speak.

It is a peaceful night in the city.
There are men and women idling through the hot
   summer streets.
Policemen lounge at every corner under the tall arc-
   lamps and dreamily swing their clubs.
Ministers are pondering sermons in their studies,
   and the Mayor is drinking lemonade at a roof-
   garden.
Judges are reading poetry aloud to their wives after
   the irritating day in court.
Lovers sit side by side in the dim movie houses and
   tingle as their bodies touch.

Mothers put their babies to bed, and father smokes
his calabash pipe.
There are a million homes so quiet that clocks fill
them with ticking,
And there are five strong detectives in a cell with a
prisoner,
And they know, by God, they can surely make him
speak.

The blackjacks rise and fall, the iron heels stamp on
the prisoner's face.
The detectives strip their wilted collars, and groan
aloud like lovers in their ecstasy.
The prisoner shuts his eyes for a moment, and sees
the million of stars that whirl in the universe
of pain,
He bites his lips until they bleed, that he may not
speak,
He prays with bloody lips that the capitalist world
he hates will never make him speak,
That the five strong detectives in the cell with him
can never, never make him speak.

THE GIRL BY THE RIVER

1.

NEW YORK is like a Negro fighter quiet after a knock-out blow,
And quiet, like a tired work-horse, the Night stands in its stall, moon-drowsing by the river.
No one loves me, nobody loves me, a young girl is moaning by the river,
As she stumbles like a drunkard through the black docks and wrings her hands by the dark river,
Alone with the stars, the locked warehouses, an old watchman and the river,
Spattering the peace with her blood, with her young hopeless passion by the river,
No one loves me! wringing her pale work hands by the dark river.

2.

O moonlight boat ride up the Hudson River when May Carty found her young taxi driver,
When he spoke soft love to her in the dark woods near the dance hall by the river,
When so beautiful and just, the man-flesh cleaved to woman-flesh, as in the world's beginning, by a river.

O Georgie, Georgie! she cried, the jazz-notes moan
    through the trees like a flight of birds lost on
    a river!
O Georgie, Georgie! I'm so lonesome in the shoe
    factory and not having no real friend but the
    river!
I could die for love, I could die in this grass with
    the wild wet smell and my sweet daddy over me,
    by the river,
O Georgie, Georgie! don't ever leave me; but he left
    her, and she bears his child by the river,
And she wanders the night docks and moans and
    wrings her hands by the dark river.

3.

We need to be loved, we droop like yellow dogs without love,
When no one loves us we plunge for peace into the
    dark river,
Old watchman, leave the property you are guarding
    and speak a word of love to the girl by the
    river.
Warehouses, smelling of spice and leather, open your
    locked doors and give her rest from the river.
Skyscrapers, stoop to her; Stars, tell her the world
    is a silver union of rivers,
Tug-boats, send her a brave yellow flare from the
    boilers as you chug down the river,
Bosses who drove her, foremen who hated her, be
    kind now, she walks by the river,

The Girl by the River

Pimps who sought to seduce her, she has come to the river at last,
Landladies, wheels, strong bankers, O factory whistles, O congressmen, O river,
O America, O you who used her, forget your money-lust now, she dreams of the river!
She is mad! she is lost! she will drown herself for want of love, in the river!
The young factory girl who moans by the dark river.

4.

I begged her to wait for dawn.
O my darling, my darling! Revolution will rise from the east on the dark river,
Bringing peace to workers, and peace to women, and no more dark river.
This is sure, this is sweet, this is stronger than strong bankers and the river.
There will be love for all, and in factories and subways, love.
It will float over the skyscrapers, and chug in the tough tug-boats down the dark river.
Wait, wait! the workers are marching over the mountains and swimming the stormy river,
The bosses cannot stop them, the old watchman cannot guard the locked doors by the river.
Wait, wait! but she would not listen, she would not understand,
She screamed and wrung her hands and plunged into the dark river.

She did not believe my words, that there would be a
    time of revolution and love,
A time of love's children conceived in woods near a
    dance hall by a river,
A time of workers' joy in boats down a gay golden
    river,
A time of no more moaning for factory girls by Life's
    loud, huge, red river.

A GREAT DEED WAS NEEDED

1.

Midnight on the hills. Black as a mine-shaft, the world. Immense, black, with shadows great as lost continents.

And a mine-lamp hangs from the sky. The huge, strong Moon. A white tower-lamp all night, lighting the great mountains.

Coal-mountains, old stone mountains that have given birth to trees, rocks, bears and men.

Peg-Leg Johnson is standing under a black tree. Look at him. He is thinking. "We gotter—we gotter—O we gotter—"

This is thinking. It hurts and chokes a miner's brain,
A miner alone in midnight on the black mountains,
A miner on strike.

2.

Peg-Leg sees soldier-tents in the dim valley. Camp-fires, too, like red and yellow play-bubbles. Or gay colored lanterns of ghouls at the miners' funeral.

"God damn them, what right have them soldiers in our town?"

Coal-diggers' town is there in the valley. Black stacks of houses down Main street, cut by a glittering sword of moon-silver. Splash of yellow lamplight. People awake in that house; a kid sick, maybe.

Human yellow lamplight sorrow splashed across the hard, white perfect moonlight.

No sounds.

Only a horse whinnying. Only a low cow-bellow, and a brooding of hens. No humans about in the moonlight.

Hush, the wind shakes the dark leaves.

No sounds, no humans about.

But there's loneliness, worry, in the frame houses on Main street.

Peg-Leg knows; it hurts his brain.

3.

Lanky Peg-Leg. Old, slow, powerful Peg-Leg, the miner.

Ancient as a coal-mountain. Storm-gnarled as a big tree on a hill. Hungry. Peg-Leg Johnson, thinker for the town of coal-diggers.

He lost his left leg in a mine explosion; yes, it was shot away, clean off.

But the stump still lives, like an unrevenged ghost; it hurts, itches, burns like mad when he is thinking.

It throbs and hurts now; Peg-Leg is thinking.

A Great Deed Was Needed

His heart goes like an automatic coal-drill. Sweat's on his face, like damp on the coal-face.

There's been four months of strike. Every one's tired and hungry. The men are hungry. The women pale as flour; hungry. The kids are like sick puppies; they don't play much; hungry.

A little beans and coffee from outside. Not enough. Cast-off clothes comin', too, but not enough. There was snow last week down the valley. Winter's comin' on, and we'll be hungry. Cold. Sick. Outside help no good any more. The soldiers are here, too. And the kids are hungry.

God, we're dyin' on our feet! The strike's cavin' in! Cowards want us to give up; crawl back to the company like yaller dogs, say we're licked. Give up the union. No! Never! The union is all we miners have got in this world. There's no God, no heaven, no justice, no country, for us miners— only the union.

And the strike's cavin' in. Cowards want to give up the union!

Never!

Kids. But the kids.

"We gotter—we gotter—we jest GOTTER do somethin'—"

What? Peg-Leg is suffering under the black tree. He sweats. He is the thinker for the town of coal-diggers.

The night ended. Then the man-trip ended. The world mine-cage shot from darkness into light. The moon-lamp flickered out, there was a bucket of smoky blood held up, poured out over the mountains.

The Sun!
Peg-Leg walked home!
His stump burned like mad!
A great deed is needed! The strike needs a great deed!

4.

Mary, my wife, the strike needs a great deed, he said.
Buddy, my miner son, the strike needs a great deed.
Come from door to door with me, come from house to house down the valley,
And before the red sun has set over the black mountains,
The strike will have had its great deed.

5.

From house to frame house, from door to screen door they went. Whispering, arguing, storming. Deep stormy words to rouse storm. Rough words, plain words in overalls, deep proletarian words. Hunger's learning, hunger's eloquence.

Come along, they said in rough words, THE STRIKE NEEDS A GREAT DEED!

Huge, hairy Jack Dorsey, and his three huge, hairy brothers, and their wives, came along. Lucky Bill Watkins, the miners' fiddler. Hilda McGregor, mother of five hungry kids, she came. Fighting Jane Hamilton in her red shawl. Poor old Kate Leith, who lost husband and sons in the mine. Many women came along.

A Great Deed Was Needed

Old Bob Shaw, with his shot-in face; it was tattooed blue in a mine explosion. Frank Hamilton, with three fingers shot off in a mine explosion. Other peg-legs, other tattooed miners, other hungry bellies and bursting hearts. They came along.

The Welsh, the Wops, the Greeks came.

Young Stanlitch, that eager boy, explained to the Hunkies in their tongue, the strike needs a great deed. And all came along.

Are you lonely, brother? Come along. You'll find comrades here.

Are you hungry, brother? Come along. We'll share your hunger.

Are you beaten, brother? Come along. We must seek for courage together.

Are you ready to die, brother? Come along, we will all die together, the strike needs a great deed.

6.

Main street at noon. Bare, cheap American Main street, familiar as a dollar bill.

But see the brave October sun. *O beautiful yellow god of the dark miners.* Courage, a fine day!

Why are the stores closed on this fine day? The show windows boarded up?

DANGER!

Business heard the alarm word ringing over the valley all morning. Business knows. DANGER! This ain't no buying crowd this morning; no groceries or shoes sold to-day.

DANGER! The coal-diggers are out for something. Muttering uneasily, in little groups, like plotters. Or forbidding and steely-hued of face, like the color of storm-clouds. Pent-up like prisoners, walking up and down the sidewalks. Or lounging against lamp-posts, spitting carefully. Waiting. Storm-clouds. DANGER!

A fire broke out in the northern end of town. The coal-diggers whispered the news up and down Main street. Desperate laughter. A desperate proletarian joke Business will never understand.

The troops were rushed to put the fire out. The miners watched the boys leave.

Now is the time!
Fall in line: we'll march on the company office!
We'll tell the superintendent we're hungry!
Every one come along!

Yes, hurry! Two thousand soldiers of poverty, fall in line. March!

Rags are the uniform, shawls and overalls. No music or drums. Unromantic army, common as daily bread. Ragged ranks of men and women shuffling common clay-dust on Main street. No banner, only the naked blue sky, the old flag of hunger. Shabby, harsh, disorderly, the shuffling regiment of the unloved poor. A mob. The sun shines on their pale, stern faces.

Peg-Leg Johnson, his white hair gleaming, stumps

A Great Deed Was Needed

in the first rank. His boy, Buddy, the young ex-soldier, marches beside him.

> *Danger! Famine in fat America! Ring the alarm bell over America, the miners are marching!*
>
> *Lawyers, beware! Legal lies won't help you now! This is famine marching!*
>
> *Landlords, barricade your tenements of profit! Justice is marching!*
>
> *Capitalists, order out the gunmen to guard your man-slaying factories! Justice is marching!*
>
> *Professors, ministers, editors, run to your holes! Poets, to your ivory towers! Reality is marching!*
>
> *Danger, O Republic, call out the troops, the miners are marching again,*
>
> *Guard yourself with cannon, O Republic, against the Justice, Truth, and Brotherly Love of the Proletariat!*

7.

They marched to the company offices. They came to the picket fence and stopped. They yelled for the Super. Nobody answered them. Then two tough gunmen came out. What do you want? they asked. Peg-Leg Johnson and Angus Hamilton stepped out of the crowd, and said, We want to speak to the Super. What do you want to tell him? a gunman asked.

We want to tell him we're hungry! said Peg-Leg Johnson.

Get the hell out of here, you big bum! said the gunman, and he tried to pull his gun.

Angus Hamilton grabbed him and threw him over the fence.

The other gunman pulled his gun, too, and fired a shot, and then ran away waving his hands like crazy. He was scared. The crowd of miners was all talking and yelling at the same time. They had a sound would scare a gunman.

The crowd was all pushing against the picket fence. What'll we do next? every one was asking at the same time. Suddenly the fence fell down *by accident*. The crowd rushed into the cinder yard, laughing and yelling like kids when school is out. There was a barbed wire fence they found there, but the coal-digger boys who had been in the army in France tore it down. *They knew how!* They showed the others how to tear barbed-wire fences down. *Sure!*

What'll we do now? every one was asking Peg-Leg Johnson and Angus Hamilton.

Let's march back!

NO! NO! NO! rattled and roared the great thunder of Justice, the voice of the mob! The storm was rising!

Then somebody said something about the company store. They went to look at it. The store was closed tight, and a big lock was on the warehouse, too. The watchman had run away.

Somebody walked up and tore the lock of the com-

A Great Deed Was Needed

pany warehouse from its staples, and threw the big warehouse doors open, wide as Justice.

The mob of coal-diggers rushed in, and grabbed everything they found there, shoes and canned beans and flour and dried pears and coffee and overalls and oatmeal and tinned milk for the kids—

They grabbed it up in their arms. Every one had enough. Every one was wild and happy over the big proletarian joke. Every one bust out singing. Some of them began eating things with a smile on their faces. The food made them drunk. It was the miners' Fourth of July.

At last Peg-Leg and Angus got them back in line again.

Let's march back and hold a big meeting in town! said Peg-Leg.

Every one is cheered up now! he yelled, we can hold the biggest meeting yet!

This strike is good for another four months now! he yelled, we can get through the winter, can't we, boys?

YES! for there has been a great deed!

8.

So the mob fell in line, they walked back, singing, laughing, and eating things as they marched in sunlight.

Listen, there were green bushes on both sides of the red clay road. At Hoyt's Corners, as they were swinging along, they came around a bend, and found the troops standing on guard among the green bushes. Listen, their rifles were up, with shiny bayonets sticking from them, like a cactus fence among the green bushes.

Halt! yelled the Captain, a fat young feller with a waxy mustache.

The coal-diggers halted. Listen, Peg-Leg Johnson stepped forward to talk to the Captain. Suddenly a hundred shots belched red from the rifles. Peg-Leg was torn to pieces with bullets. He fell into the red clay road. Listen, blood came out of him. Red blood was on his face, and his white hair. Listen, there was a lot of his blood. Peg-Leg's boy Buddy rushed to help him, but it was too late. Peg-Leg had died for the coal-diggers. About thirty other miners were wounded, and ten women and three kids. Listen, brother, there was plenty of blood on the green bushes and the red clay road.

9.

Midnight on the hills.

Black as a mine-shaft, the world.

The huge moon shines on the coal-mountains.

Under the black tree where Peg-Leg Johnson used to stand, another miner is standing. It is Peg-Leg's son, Buddy.

"We gotter—we gotter—O we gotter—"

He is thinking. It hurts and chokes the brain of a young miner who first begins to think.

He remembers England, France. His three years in war. Democracy. Wilson. The Kaiser. The

A Great Deed Was Needed

lives of the poor in England, France, Germany, too.

Those coal-diggers in those other countries—are they up against our kind of fight, too? he asked the Moon.

He was weeping for his brave father. He was shivering. He wanted to shoot somebody. He was crazy. He was bitter as poison. He wanted another war. He wanted dynamite. He wanted books to read. He wanted to know how to do something big. He wanted a big revenge. He wanted earthquake, flood and fire over fat America. He wanted to run amuck. He wanted to think.

The night ended over the black tree.
Red flood and red fire swept in over America.
The Sun.
Buddy Johnson walked home, shouting,
The whole world needs a great deed, he shouted at the Sun,
This world needs a great proletarian deed, he shouted,
Men of England! Men of France! Men of Germany! Men of America! The world needs a great proletarian deed!

STRIKE!

A Mass Recitation

Foreword

Mass Recitation in Soviet Russia, as in Germany, is very popular with the workers. Mass Recitation is one of the most powerful and original forms developed in the struggle for proletarian culture. It is art that has grown out of the workers' life and needs; it is useful art.

Mass Recitation is like great oratory; it is a valuable weapon for propaganda and solidarity. I have tried to write a Mass Recitation for the needs of American workers, and I hope other proletarian writers will experiment in the form, and workers' dramatic groups produce their experiments.

The rough bare platform of any ordinary union hall or meeting hall is enough, is the most fitting stage, in fact, for a Mass Recitation.

About thirty men and women are needed in the one that follows. As indicated, they are scattered in groups or as individuals through the audience. Except for those who take the parts of Capitalists, Police, etc., they are dressed in their usual street clothes; they have no make-up on, there is nothing to distinguish them from their fellow-workers in the audience.

Strike! 171

This is what makes a Mass Recitation so thrilling and real. The action in my recitation commences on the platform, with POVERTY speaking; suddenly from the midst of the audience a group of men workers chant; then a woman stands up and shouts something; then a group of girls in another part of the house.

The audience is taken by surprise; they cannot guess who may be sitting next to them; they are kept on the *qui vive* as from this corner and that corner, perhaps from the quiet persons next to them dramatic voices are lifted and workers like themselves rise to shout passionate slogans or to storm the platform. The audience is swept more and more into the excitement all around them; they become one with the actors, a real mass; before the recitation is over, every one in the hall should be shouting: Strike! Strike!

A Mass Recitation needs a good director, very careful rehearsals, and an exact sense of spacing and rhythm. The lines must be chanted, not spoken; in clear full sculptured tones, each word as sharply defined as a rifle shot—what Meyerhold calls "poster-declamation." No hurry; the vowels strongly emphasized. Mass recitations are delivered in the heroic style.

Above all, no individualism; the director must find the rhythm of the whole recitation and discipline each word and each actor to the general plan.

SCENE: *A platform with a long table and chairs.*

POVERTY, *a gaunt woman in rags, with a strange white face of hunger, comes slowly on the platform. She sits down in one of the chairs.*

WEALTH *enters next, pompously, a fat gross figure like a capitalist, with a sensual mask.*

Music may accompany each of these figures as they enter.

WEALTH (*gruffly*): Who are you?
Were you invited?
POVERTY (*calmly*): I was not invited.
WEALTH: Why present then?
Go, ragged woman.
POVERTY: I am Poverty, your sister.
I go where you go.
WEALTH (*furiously*): Lie, lie, lie!
Poverty is not my sister.
POVERTY (*calmly*): Greed is our father.
WEALTH (*shouting*): Go, ragged woman.
I will call my dogs.
POVERTY (*coldly*): So have you always answered me,
With your soldiers and police.
A MAN FROM THE MASS (*solemnly*): We are suffering.
A WOMAN: Our children hunger.
CHORUS: Give us bread.
(*No response from* WEALTH. *He has turned to greet four* DIRECTORS, *capitalists, fat and rubbing their hands. They come and stand about the table.*)
DIRECTORS (*skipping gayly and clasping hands in a*

childish dance around WEALTH): Good morning, good morning, good morning!
God's in his heaven,
Dollars on earth,
All's right with the world!
All's well, all's well!

WEALTH: Let us pray, gentlemen.

(*They pray with folded hands, and lifted faces.*)

DIRECTORS: Give us this day our daily cake, our daily lobsters and champagne, our nightly chorus girls and cabarets. For ours is the power and glory on earth. Forever and ever, Amen.

1ST DIRECTOR (*frowning heavily*): But who is this ragged woman?

2ND DIRECTOR: She is positively not a member of our Board of Directors.

DIRECTORS: No, no!

1ST DIRECTOR: In rags.

2ND: Common.

3RD: Needs food.

4TH: A failure.

1ST: Who is she?

WEALTH: She is Poverty.
She wishes to speak
To the Board of Directors.

DIRECTORS (*angrily*): Poverty? Can't be!

1ST DIRECTOR: Impostor.

2ND DIRECTOR: Illegal in America.

3RD DIRECTOR: Her own fault.

4TH DIRECTOR: She should save her wages. Thrift.

1ST DIRECTOR: To the hoosegow.
Poverty is criminal. We are respectable.

WEALTH (*sneering*): You have your answer, Poverty. Go, not a word here!

(POVERTY *rises with dignity, and goes to other part of platform, where she stands with folded arms.*)

MAN IN THE MASS (*deeply*): We are suffering.

WOMAN: Our children are cold.

GIRL: We cannot live.

ANOTHER MAN: Our sun has set.

ANOTHER WOMAN: Who will listen to us?

CHORUS OF BASSOS: Night on the workers, night on their houses.

CHORUS OF SOPRANOS: Yet we *must* live.

TENORS: We *must* live.

CONTRALTOS: We must.

BASSOS: We must.

CHORUS OF ALL: We must, we must, the workers *must* live!

(*The* DIRECTORS *pretend not to have heard. They fuss with papers and documents they take from their pockets, and sit down at the table in unison.*)

WEALTH (*standing as chairman*): Gentlemen, as chairman of this annual meeting of the Board of Directors

I beg to report our corporation has had a most profitable year.

DIRECTORS (*pulling out little American flags and waving them*): Hurrah! A most profitable year!

CHORUS (*solemnly*): We live in darkness.

WEALTH: We can report an increase in profits
Of twelve million, seven hundred thousand

Eight hundred forty dollars and nine cents.
DIRECTORS (*as before*): Banzai! Banzai!
Eight hundred forty dollars,
And nine cents.
CHORUS: Who will listen to us?
WEALTH: Many new machines were installed,
Many improvements made,
We glitter with efficiency for the new fiscal year,
Our engineers are modern heroes.
DIRECTORS: Viva! Viva! Modern heroes!
CHORUS: Our children have no bread.
WEALTH: And we look to an even more successful year.
The nation is booming, booming, gentlemen,
We have captured many foreign markets,
America is king of the world.
DIRECTORS: Hoch, hoch! Viva. Banzai. Hurrah.
King of the world.
CHORUS OF WOMEN: But the toilers cannot live.
CHORUS OF MEN: Night on the toilers, night on their houses.
WEALTH: And in conclusion, in order to insure even greater profits,
I would seriously recommend, gentlemen,
That we cut the wages of our workers
Ten Per Cent
All in favor say *Aye*.
DIRECTORS (*leaping to their feet, and prancing and shouting in a delirium of joy*): Aye, aye, aye.
Hurrah!
Ten Per Cent! Ten Per Cent!
Yachts, strings of pearls!

Chorus girls, Florida holidays!
Ten Per Cent! Ten Per Cent!
Champagne! Charity! Rolls-Royce!

WEALTH (*shouting*): The vote is carried.

(*They go out, embracing each other in drunken joy.*)

WEALTH (*a last triumphant shout*): The world is ours!

DIRECTORS: Ten Per Cent. Hooray!

(*There is a dead silence after they leave.* POVERTY *steps slowly to center of platform.*)

POVERTY (*solemnly*): Ten Per Cent.
Words of fate.
Words of hunger and death. (*Pause.*)

A WOMAN (*tearfully*): A cut in wages is a cut at our lives.
I work in the mills by night, my husband by day.
Yet we cannot live.

CHORUS: We cannot live.

A MAN (*bitterly*): Cheap shoes, cheap clothes, cheap houses,
Cheap common food our lot.
A straw on a stormy sea
We have clutched at our wages.
Now the bosses unclasp our fingers.
We will drown!

CHORUS: We will drown. (*Pause.*)

MAN (*desperately*): Can we bear it?
I cannot bear it.
Suffering is heaped up in me like gunpowder.
Bring no match near.
I cannot bear it! (*Pause.*)

Strike!

CHORUS: We cannot bear it. (*Pause.*)
POVERTY: Ten Per Cent.
  Scorpion draining the breasts of mothers.
  Leech sucking men's blood.
  Ten Per Cent—bread for workers.
  Now diamonds for bosses. (*Pause.*)
MAN: I will not bear it.
  I came to America for freedom,
  But I am slave to a machine.
A WOMAN: My baby is ill.
  And no one cares.
AN OLD WORKER: After a life of toil,
  I die to-morrow
  In the poorhouse.
  So shall you all end.
CHORUS OF SOPRANOS: Is there no joy for us,
  No spring for youth?
  The world for the rich?
CHORUS OF TENORS: Is the blue sky for bosses,
CHORUS OF BASSOS: Something must be done.
A MAN: Our hour has come.
CHORUS OF CONTRALTOS: Something must be done.
CHORUS OF ALL (*with deep conviction*): For the workers *must* live. (*Pause.*)
  (*A woman rises.*)
POVERTY: Defeated woman worker,
  Speak!
WOMAN (*feebly*): We are so weak, we workers.
  Too huge our fate.
  What can be done?
  Let us submit.

CHORUS OF WOMEN: Shame!
(*A man rises.*)
POVERTY: Defeated man worker.
Speak!
MAN (*feebly*): Old and defeated,
I shall die in the poorhouse.
How can I struggle?
Let us submit.
WOMAN (*fearfully*): For bosses have judges.
MAN: Bosses have police.
CHORUS: Shame. (*Pause.*)
WOMAN: Bosses have wealth.
MAN: Bosses have church.
CHORUS: Shame. (*Pause.*)
WOMAN: Bosses have newspapers.
MAN: Bosses have government.
CHORUS: Shame. (*Pause.*)
WOMAN: And we have nothing.
MAN: And we are so weak.
WOMAN: We are life's victims.
MAN: Yes, let us submit. (*Pause.*)
CHORUS: Shame, shame!
POVERTY: For the workers *must* live. (*Pause.*)
CHORUS: We must, we must, the workers *must* live!
(*Defeated man and woman come to platform, stumbling and pitiful, and moaning like lost sheep.*)
MAN AND WOMAN: Defeated, defeated!
Lost, lost, let us submit!
Who can help the workers?
Only God can help.

Strike!

Let us pray.

(*One is at each end of platform, and they kneel.*)

MAN AND WOMAN: Our Father, which art in heaven, give us this day our daily bread. Forgive us our trespasses, as we forgive those who trespass against us, for——

A YOUNG LEADER IN THE MASS: Shame!

MAN AND WOMAN (*timidly*): For Thine is the power——

YOUNG LEADER: Shame! Ours the power!

BASSOS: Ours the power!

A GIRL: And ours the glory.

SOPRANOS: Ours the glory.

(*Pause. Defeated man and woman look about them timidly. They start to mumble their prayer again, but are interrupted.*)

MAN AND WOMAN: Forever and ever——

YOUNG LEADER (*rushing to platform, and shouting in powerful tones*):

Up from your knees.

God is a capitalist.

He will not help us.

We must help ourselves.

(*Man and Woman rise from their knees.*)

MAN: Then what's to be done?

WOMAN: Are we not weak?

CHORUS: Something must be done.

YOUNG LEADER (*springing on platform*): Strike!

CHORUS (*repeating confusedly*): Strike? Strike?

DEFEATED WOMAN: But bosses have police.

YOUNG LEADER (*sternly*): Strike!

We fought in their war.

Workers have no fear.
Strike! Strike!

MAN AND WOMAN (*leaving platform*): But bosses have judges. Bosses have wealth. Bosses have all. We have nothing.

YOUNG LEADER: Strike!
Workers have each other.
Who moves the wheels?

CHORUS: We move the wheels.

YOUNG LEADER: Strike!
Stop the wheels
And profits stop.
Who are the masses?

CHORUS: We are the masses.

YOUNG LEADER: Strike!
Stand together in masses,
In solidarity,
And the bosses are beaten.
Who owns the world?

CHORUS: We own the world!

YOUNG LEADER: Strike!
Strike for the world.
Strike for the new.
Strike for the future.
Strike, strike!

CHORUS (*at full power*): Strike! Strike! Strike!
(WEALTH *appears, puffing and angry.*)

WEALTH (*screaming*): Sedition!
Who shouts Strike!

CHORUS: We shout Strike!

WEALTH: You were contented till he came.
Mad dog, traitor.

Do you know who he is?

CHORUS: He is a worker.

WEALTH (*screaming*): He is an Agitator!

CHORUS (*greeting this with ribald laughter*): Ho, ho, ho! Strike! Strike!

WEALTH: Arrest that man. (*He whistles and police appear.*) Arrest that Bolshevik! (*Four burlesque policemen surround the young leader. Pause.*)

YOUNG LEADER (*boldly*): Arrest me, but hunger is not arrested.

Arrest me, but low wages are not arrested.

Strike, strike!

WEALTH: Take him to prison.

(*Four young men and four young women come up to platform, while chorus chants—*)

CHORUS: No, no!

EIGHT YOUNG WORKERS (*coming on platform and speaking with deep menace*): He is our leader,

Do not attack him,

Bone of our bone,

Son of the masses.

A YOUNG WORKER: Release him at once.

(*The police stand back.*)

CHORUS: This is our leader.

Voice of the masses.

Bone of our bone.

WEALTH: Do you defy the law?

EIGHT YOUNG WORKERS: Yes. (*Close in around the leader with joined hands, leaving the cops outside the circle.*)

1ST COP (*moving off*): Goddamn, no law and order!

2ND COP: Goddamn, too many to be clubbed!
3RD COP: Goddamn, the country is ruined!
4TH COP: Goddamn, let's git the tear gas!
CHORUS (*jeering*): Boo-oo-oo! Scabs! (*The cops disappear.*)
WEALTH (*mad with rage*): Our judges will jail you.
Our papers revile you.
CHORUS: Strike!
WEALTH: Your women will weep.
Your children starve.
We will teach you, we will teach you,
America is mine!
CHORUS: Boo-oo-oo! Scab, scab, scab! (WEALTH *escapes amid the booing with grotesque gestures of rage. Pause.*)
POVERTY (*taking leader's hand*): Voice of the toilers,
Son of the masses,
Lead us to victory,
Too long have we suffered.
YOUNG LEADER (*solemnly*): Here is my heart's blood.
My dreams and my manhood.
Faithful I march with you,
Into the new.
FOUR YOUNG MEN (*on platform*): The masses follow you.
FOUR YOUNG WOMEN: The masses love you.
CHORUS: The masses arise.
YOUNG LEADER: The masses will be free. (*Pause.*)
Strike!
CHORUS: Strike!
On to victory.
MAN'S VOICE (*angrily*): Too long have we suffered.

Strike! 183

WOMAN (*fiercely*): Ten per cent is death.
BASSOS (*triumphantly*): Dawn for the workers.
SOPRANOS (*heroically*): Struggle and victory!
POVERTY (*joyously*): Strike, strike!
YOUNG LEADER: Strike!
EIGHT YOUNG WORKERS: Strike!
CHORUS: Strike, strike, strike, strike, strike!

(*They shout this to a climax, but while the male section is shouting this rhythmically, the women break into the last part of the chorus of the Internationale.*)

'Tis the final conflict,
Let each stand in his place,
The International Soviet
Shall be the human race.

(*The whole audience rises, and the male part of the chorus starts the beginning of the Internationale:*)

Arise, ye prisoners of starvation—

(*There are rhythmic shouts of* Strike, Strike *scattered all through the singing, and timed dramatically like a drum beat.*)

VANZETTI IN THE DEATH HOUSE

A Worker's Recitation*

(In his chains and prison suit, Vanzetti paces the dark cell)

One-two-three-four.
I count the steps like a miser.
One-two-three-four.
Up and down the cell, but I can find no peace.
In my heart, venom; in my brain, fire!
Doomed!
One-two-three-four!
We are doomed, Sacco and I!
We are in the death house at last!
Doomed!
One-two-three-four!

(He sits, puts his face between his hands, speaks bitterly)

After seven years of struggle, of unspeakable anguish,
To be in this dungeon without stars.
Waiting for the last farce of justice,
The three shocks in the electric chair!

(He stands and paces nervously)

I am not afraid to die.
I will walk my road to the end.
I will remain a rebel and a lover.

---

* This recitation is based on the published speeches and letters of Vanzetti. Almost every line is a verbatim extract.

I will remain true to the working class.
I am in the hands of the tyrants,
Let them crucify me!
One-two-three-four.
> *(He sits down wearily)*

For I am tired, tired, tired.
For seven years I have drunk their vinegar and gall.
All my life I have drunk their poison and poverty.
I am tired of this capitalist world.
Come, Death!
> *(He regards his chains)*

Oh, capitalist system, I know you well.
I have heard the prayers of your starving children.
I have heard the groans of your young dying soldiers.
I have seen the agony of strong men hunting for jobs.
I know your crimes, capitalism, I know your crazy houses,
Your jails, factories and hospitals filled with victims!
You are a monster, I hate you,
I am glad to die!
> *(He drops his head between his arms bitterly)*

They prepare a new world war.
They prepare new slaveries for the masses.
They prepare new jails.
They prepare new frame-ups,
New electric chairs!
> *(He springs up, he shouts in a red rage:)*

Fiends!

Ghouls!
Assassins of the poor!
Blood-drinkers!
We will have revenge!
Revolution!
Give me a million men,
And I will walk from this jail
And set America free!
> *(He collapses on the bench. Then in a low voice:)*

Vanzetti, be still.
Be steady, my strong heart.
Truth has ever been your god.
Look into the eyes of Truth now, Vanzetti,
And read your fate.
You are doomed, Vanzetti.
The businessmen thirst for your blood.
The Christians thirst for your blood.
Remember Governor Fuller!
Remember Judge Thayer!
They thirst for workers' blood!
> *(He leaps up with a bitter cry:)*

Not a scorpion, not a snake,
Not a leprous dog would they have dealt with so!
Murderers!
> *(He paces a moment, then lifts his fists despairingly)*

But my Italy is in the death house, too,
Mussolini is her Judge Thayer,
Her murderer, O my Italy!
> *(He sits on the bench, looks at a photograph)*

Vanzetti in the Death House

They sent me this picture of my native village,
To cheer me in the death house.
O my Italy, it is hard to die!
O my native village, I have never forgotten you,
My father's garden, and my father's vineyards,
And the guitars playing, the mountain boys singing,
The smell of fruit, and the glorious sun on my face,
O my Italy, it is hard to die!

(He kisses the picture, puts it away. He stares into space, his voice is tender)

Now I work in my father's garden again.
It is all so unspeakably beautiful in Italy.
The fig trees are in bloom, the cherry trees, plums, apricots, peaches.
The grape arbors, the potato vines, I can see them all,
And all those dear, humble vegetables of the poor,
The red and yellow peppers, the parsley and onions!
O my Italy, it is hard to die!

(He looks up. His voice is like music)

There were singing birds there:
The black merles, with golden beak,
Their sweet song even more golden,
And the orioles, and the chaffinches,
And the nightingales of Italy,
Most beautiful over all, O nightingales!

(He gazes at the ground, his voice trembles)

And there were nations of flowers, too.
In my father's garden were wild daisies and forget-me-nots.
And blue violets lived there, and the white and red clover,

And other scented, rainbow flowers,
Under the blue sky of my Italy.
> *(He clasps his hands and speaks with a lover's sorrow)*

O Mother Nature, have I not always adored you?
Was I not ever your loving son,
So rich in mind and love I needed no money?
Needing only a roof, a few books, and some comrades,
A crust of bread and Liberty,
And wind and sun, my Mother?
> *(He stands and paces the cell. Then with tragic fierceness:)*

But I loved Humanity more, O my Mother.
The world misery tore at my heart.
In proletarian hells, in jails and factories,
I beheld the crucifixion of the poor.
And I worked, I preached with all my heart
That the social wealth belong to all,
That Humanity be free,
And this was my crime, O Mother,
For this they locked me here,
To wait for my death,
To wait for my murderers.
> *(He shouts with hate and horror:)*

For Fuller and Thayer!
> *(He paces the cell in passionate silence. It takes him six turns of the cell to grow calm. Then he sits, and says in a strange, resolute voice:)*

Be calm, Vanzetti.
The price of perfection is a high and sorrowful one.
They will burn your body in the electric chair,

Vanzetti in the Death House 189

But your ideas will live.
The working class will be free.
Mother Nature whispers it to you.
>*(He speaks mysteriously, a man in a trance:)*

The chains are loose, I walk freely out of my cell,
I climb the snow mountains above my native village,
I dive in the stream of living water,
I drink at the cold Alpine springs,
I climb on, and reach the highest peaks,
And see the lands, waters, sky of my Italy!
>*(He rises, he holds his hands forward)*

Farewell, Italy, my native village and beloved folk.
Farewell, crucified working class of the world.
Farewell, sun and wind and sky, and little flowers I have loved.
Farewell, America of many wheels and cruel Christians.
I accept my destiny, O Governor,
America, I accept thy electric chair!
>*(He then flings his arms backward in the position of one crucified, saying with slow, solemn courage:)*

Yes.
Yes.
This is my career and triumph.
If it had not been for this thing,
I might have lived out my life talking at street corners to scornful men.
I might have died unmarked, unknown,
A failure.
Sacco, we are not a failure now.
Comrade, this is our career and triumph,

Never in life could we have hoped
To do such good for the working class
As we do now by dying.
Governor Fuller, take our lives,
Lives of a good shoemaker and poor fish peddler—
That last moment will belong to us—
That last agony is our triumph—
The workers will never forget—
    (He flings up his arms and chants solemnly:)
LONG LIVE THE REVOLUTION!

120 MILLION

They told me to love my country, America.
But where is America?
I saw no nation in my wandering between the oceans.
I saw 120 millions,
And they hated each other,
And they slugged each other,
In a war for money.

America is not one,
It is many.
The white man burns the Negro alive.
The mill boss whips little children.
The army shoots down miners.
The army shoots down weavers.
It is a land of enemies.

I saw the sun walk over the Rocky Mountains.
I saw the wheatfields blaze in the plains.
I saw millions of American flowers,
And heard the birdsong of America.
It is a strong and beautiful earth,
And I, a worker, loved it,
But how could I love those who kill workers?

America, I cannot worship your Money God,
This monster whose heart is a Ford car,
Whose brain is a cheap Hollywood movie,
Whose cities are mad mechanical nightmares,

Whose litany is of fur coats and silk stockings,
Whose worshipers die of nervous glut,
Whose victims die of hunger.

Who killed Sacco and Vanzetti?
Not you, O Mississippi River.
Who extorted the world's gold?
Not you, O Allegheny Mountains.
Who killed Germans for profit?
Not you, O American fields and forests.

It is a strong and beautiful earth,
But the world hates its new tyrant.
Europe and Asia prepare a war,
It will come, the ruin, defeat and sorrow,
For you, fat America.
And Lenin will walk among your 120 million,
Sooner or later, Lenin.
First or last, Lenin.
Lenin! Lenin!

Lenin!
I see the bloody birth you will bring.
I see fire and ashes,
And my own land rising from the ashes.
I see peace for the 120 million.
I see a Hammer-Sun by day,
A Sickle-Moon by night,
Shining on a new America,
A Workers' and Farmers' America.

THE END